nickelodeon

BIG NATE

NEXT STOP, SUPERSTARDOM!

Inspired by the comics and
book series by Lincoln Peirce

Based on the episodes written by
Michael Ryan, Lissy Klatchko,
and Emily Brundige

Andrews McMeel
PUBLISHING®

Andrews McMeel Publishing
a division of Andrews McMeel Universal
1130 Walnut Street, Kansas City, Missouri 64106

www.andrewsmcmeel.com

Book design, layout, and lettering by The Story Division
www.thestorydivision.com

Editor: Lucas Wetzel
Designer: Niko Dalcin
Cover Design: Spencer Williams
Production Editor: Dave Shaw
Production Manager: Chuck Harper

Special thanks to:
Jeff Whitman, Jarrin Jacobs, and Nathan Schram at Nickelodeon
Steffie Davis, Steve Osgoode, and Niko Dalcin at The Story Division
And special thanks to Lincoln Peirce for editorial guidance throughout this project.

23 24 25 26 27 SDB 10 9 8 7 6 5 4 3 2 1

ISBN (paperback): 978-1-5248-7931-0
ISBN (hardcover): 978-1-5248-8415-4

Library of Congress Control Number: 2022950384

Made by:
RR Donnelley (Guangdong) Printing Solutions Company Ltd
Address and location of manufacturer:
No. 2, Minzhu Road, Daning, Humen Town,
Dongguan City, Guangdong Province, China 523930
1st Printing – 1/2/23

CONTENTS

ULTRA-NATE

The Ghostly Coven of Man Witches

Chapter 1
A PERFECT DAY
PS88

I AM **LOVING** THIS MORNING! IT'S ONE OF THOSE DAYS WHERE **NOTHING** CAN GO WRONG!

OH NO!
A DAY WHEN YOU SMILE AT THE WORLD AND THE WORLD SMILES BACK!
CLONK!

NAB!

NICE SAVE, NATE!

A BEAUTIFUL DAY!

URGH!

CLICK!

CLAP!
CLAP!

A PERFECT DAY!

WHAP!
SMACK!

LET'S GO!

LIFE IS SO, **SO** GOOD! I MEAN, WHAT COULD ***POSSIBLY*** GO WRONG ON SUCH A BEAUTIFUL DAY?

TEST!

NOOOOOOOOOOOOOOOOO!

OH, PLEASE, PLEASE, ***PLEASE*** MAKE THIS TEST GO AWAY!

UMM, NATE, WHO ARE YOU TALKING TO?
ANYBODY WHO WILL LISTEN!

OH, NATE, NOW IT REALLY ***IS*** A BEAUTIFUL DAY! JUST WATCHING YOU FAIL...

...IT'S THE MOST GLORIOUS MOMENT OF MY YOUNG LIFE!

CHILD
VILLAIN
ACADEMIC

STUFF A SOCK IN IT, GINA! FOR YOUR INFORMATION, I ***ALMOST*** STUDIED...BUT I GOT A LITTLE DISTRACTED... REPEATEDLY.

YOUR GOOSE IS ***COOKED,*** AND I'M ENJOYING THE CRACKLINS!

MWAHAHAHAHAHAHA!!

TEST
YOU FAIL!

GROAN!

EARTH
PFFFFFT!

YOU BOYS READY FOR THE BIG MIDDLE SCHOOL BAKE OFF?
HECK YEAH! WE'RE GONNA TAKE IT THIS YEAR!
P.S. 38 SURE COULD USE THE **PRIZE MONEY** FROM THAT COMPETITION!
WE ARE **NOT** LOSING THIS YEAR TO...

JEFFERSON MIDDLE SCHOOL!

⋟GROAN!⋞ IT'S THEIR PRINCIPAL!
THAT DEMON, MRS. ZAGORAC, ALWAYS WINS WITH HER EVIL BUT **OH-SO-DELICIOUS** CRAB CAKE LOBSTER MUFFINS!

HOW DOES SHE DO IT? EVERY YEAR SHE WINS ANOTHER TROPHY FOR...

JEFFERSON MIDDLE SCHOOL!

POSITIVITY, GENTLEMEN! THIS YEAR IS OURS!

"LIKE SUDDENLY, THE SCHOOL IS ***MAGICALLY*** TELEPORTED TO THE MOON!

PS38

WHOOOOMMMM!

FWIP!

PHWOOMP!

"...AND NO ONE CAN HEAR YOU STUDY IN SPACE!

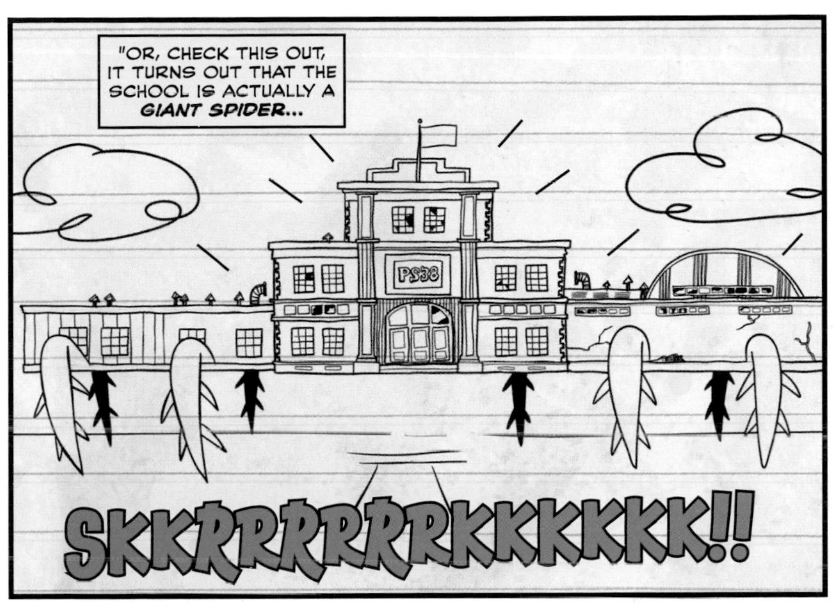
"OR, CHECK THIS OUT, IT TURNS OUT THAT THE SCHOOL IS ACTUALLY A *GIANT SPIDER*...
PS38
SKKRRRRRRKKKKKK!!

"...AND IT DECIDES TO TAKE OFF AND MAKE A NEW HOME IN THE HIMALAYAS!

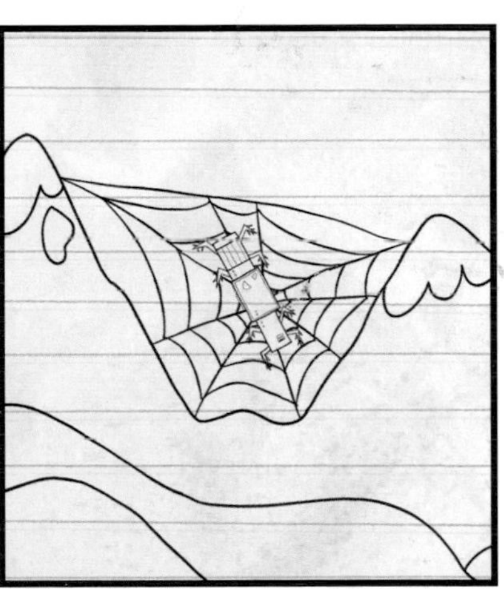

"I MEAN HEY, THE SCHOOL IS LIVING ITS TRUE AUTHENTIC SELF! IT'S PRETTY SWEET!"

OKAY, YEAH, THESE ARE GREAT! BUT HOW THE HECK CAN I MAKE THEM HAPPEN?

YOU KNOW, NATE, YOU COULD JUST ***STUDY.***

ZIP IT, GINA! STUDYING IS ***NOT*** THE ANSWER! IT'S ***TOO LATE*** FOR THAT.

OH, NATE. YOU ARE CORRECT! IT IS DEFINITELY FAR TOO LATE... MWAHAHA!

SIGH!

AFTER SCHOOL.

ARGH! I JUST DON'T UNDERSTAND IT...
THERE IS SOMETHING ***NOT QUITE RIGHT*** ABOUT THESE SOUFFLÉS.

ELLEN, WOULD YOU ***MIND?*** I CAN'T HEAR MY INNER FEELINGS OF CRUSHING PANIC AND DESPAIR OVER HERE!

HEY, DORKUS, STOP COMPLAINING AND LET ME BORROW YOUR MOUTH HOLE!
NOPE, NOT INTERESTED!

IT'S FOR YOUR SCHOOL. I VOLUNTEERED TO HELP YOUR TEACHERS WITH THE BIG MIDDLE SCHOOL BAKE-OFF!
I MEAN, THEY NEED ALL THE HELP THEY CAN GET GOING UP AGAINST...

JEFFERSON MIDDLE SCHOOL!

JUST TASTE IT!
NOPE.
COME ON.
NO!
WHAT IS WRONG WITH YOU? BESIDES THE OBVIOUS STUFF.

LOOK, I HAVE A BIG TEST TOMORROW...
ZWIP!
GULP!

MMM.
MM.
YEAH.

YEAH. NO.
HERE'S YOUR
PROBLEM.

YOU PUT IN TOO MUCH CREAM OF TARTAR AND YOU LET YOUR EGG WHITES GET DRY, RESULTING IN A DISTINCT LACK OF FLUFFINESS!

HOW DO YOU KNOW SO MUCH ABOUT BAKING?

YOU REMEMBER THAT SUMMER WHEN I SET OUT TO DISCOVER THE SECRET OF THE ***WORLD'S MOST PERFECT*** CUPCAKES?

MWHAHAHAHA!

IF IT WAS SO PERFECT, ***WHY*** DIDN'T YOU SAVE THE RECIPE?

THE WORLD IS NOT READY FOR A PERFECT CUPCAKE, ELLEN! I HAD TO DESTROY IT. IN MY COLON.

GASP!

TA-DAHHHHHH!

AHHHHHH!

HEY KIDS. IT'S ME!

YOUR DAD!
POP!

DAD, WHAT ARE YOU DOING? YOU COULD HAVE RUINED MY SOUFFLÉS!

AHH, THEY'RE OKAY! THEY'RE PERFECT!

BLOOP!

I KNOW I'LL REGRET ASKING THIS, BUT...WHY ARE YOU DRESSED LIKE A CLOWN, DAD?

WELL, SON, IT'S KIND OF SAD, REALLY. AN OLDER MEMBER OF MY BOWLING TEAM PASSED AWAY.
HE WAS AN AMATEUR CLOWN.
AND, AS A TRIBUTE, ME AND MY BOWLING BUDDIES DECIDED TO ALL ATTEND THE FUNERAL IN CLOWN COSTUMES!

NEAT, HUH? DON'T I MAKE A GREAT CLOWN?
HONK! HONK!

DAD, I GOTTA SAY, YOU REALLY SCARED US!
WAIT A MINUTE...

...YOU REALLY, ***REALLY*** SCARED US!

Chapter 2
THE PLAN
ALL RIGHT, HERE'S THE PLAN, GUYS...

WE'RE GOING TO SHUT DOWN THE SCHOOL BY CONVINCING EVERYONE...

...IT'S *HAUNTED!*

IT'S NOT THAT FAR-FETCHED.
HERE IN RACKLEFF, WE HAVE A HISTORY OF WITCHCRAFT.
BUT NOBODY KNOWS ABOUT IT!

INCLUDING *US!*
YEAH, WHAT ARE YOU TALKING ABOUT?

RACKLEFF A HISTORY
YEARS AGO, A GHOSTLY COVEN OF MAN-WITCHES HAUNTED THE VILLAGE OF RACKLEFF...

...KIDNAPPING CHILDREN...
Man-Witches

...AND COOKING THEM IN THEIR CAULDRONS!

JUST THINKING ABOUT IT MAKES MY REFLUX— GAG!

BLARGHHH!

IT'S A GOOD THING I'M HERE! SCARY PERFORMANCES ARE MY SPECIALTY!

I ONCE HAD THE **STARRING ROLE** IN EDGAR ALLAN POE'S "THE TELL-TALE HEART"...
...A STAGE ADAPTATION I CREATED, WROTE, DIRECTED, DID THE COSTUMES, CATERING, STAGE MANAGING...
...AND MY FAVORITE PART WAS THAT I PLAYED THE HEART THAT WAS THUMPING AWAY UNDER THE FLOORBOARDS...

THUMP THUMP...THUMP THUMP...

UNFORTUNATELY, NO ONE READ THE REVIEWS BECAUSE IT WAS BACK IN PRESCHOOL AND NOBODY COULD READ YET.

I, FOR ONE, WAS ***VERY*** MOVED AT YOUR REHEARSAL!

ALL RIGHT GUYS, ***OPERATION NO TEST*** IS A GO!

LET'S DECORATE! BY THE TIME SCHOOL ROLLS AROUND TOMORROW, P.S. 38 WILL BE THE ***SCARIEST*** PLACE IN TOWN!

CREAK!

I **SEE** YOU, NATE WRIGHT! YOU WILL NOT WEASEL YOUR WAY OUT OF TOMORROW'S TEST WITH SOME CRAZY PLAN!
I WILL NOT ALLOW IT! I WILL **STOP** YOU!

SMOOSH!

EW!

PS38

HISTORICAL SITE
THE HORRID COVEN OF MAN-WITCHES OF RACKLEFF WERE TRIED, SENTENCED, AND EXECUTED ON THIS VERY SPOT WHERE PS38 NOW STANDS. GO BOBCATS!
WHOA, LOOK AT THIS!

FUNNY, I NEVER NOTICED THAT PLAQUE BEFORE.
IT'S GIVING ME THE CREEPIES!

KEEP IT STEALTHY, TEAM!

CREEEEAK!

SHOOP!

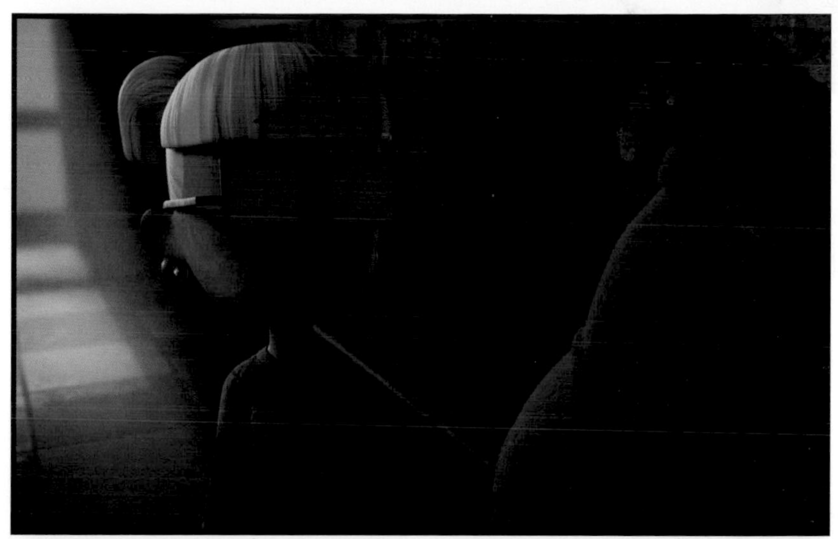
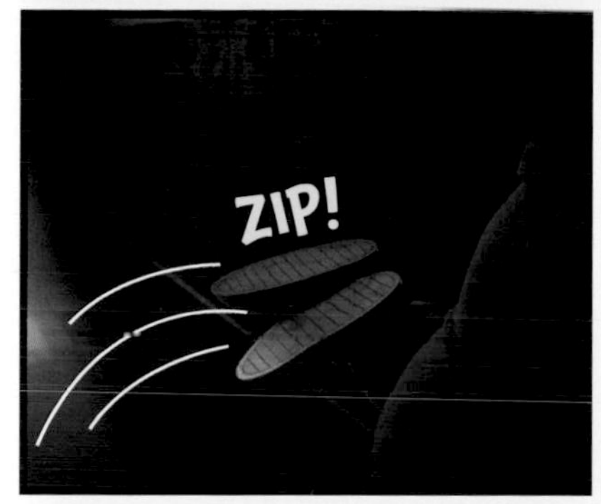
ZIP!

CLUNK!

SMOOSH!

EW!

BEEP!

TIME TO SCARE OUR WAY TO ***NO TEST! MWAHAHA!***

BOO!
AHHHH!

HAHAHA!

HM? HAHA!

BLARG!

TO **SCARE** OR ***NOT TO SCARE***, THAT IS THE QUESTION!

GRUNT!

OH, YEAH! THIS IS LOOKING REALLY GOOD.

DEFINITELY GONNA SEND EVERYONE RUNNING FROM THE SCHOOL IN TERROR TOMORROW MORNING...
...AND THEN- NO TEST! HA...

-CHAAA!
I KNOW. I'M SCARED ALREADY! HEEHEE!

CHAD, WHAT ARE YOU **DOING** HERE?

I HAVE NO IDEA!
ALL RIGHT, WELL, YOU CAN STAY, 'CAUSE YOU'RE CUTE.

AWWW, YOU'RE LIKE OUR LITTLE MASCOT. COME HERE, COME HERE!

PANT! PANT!
AWWW, WHO'S A LITTLE CUTIE?!
HEEHEE! THANKS, GUYS!

OOOOOOOOOOOOOOOO!
GASP!
YOU HEAR THAT?!

DID ONE OF YOU SET UP A SOUND MACHINE?
THAT'S **NOT OURS**, NATE!
OOOOOOOOOOOOOOO!

OOOOOOOOOOOOO!

WHOOMMMMM!
THAT DOESN'T MAKE ANY SENSE!
THESE OLD RADIATORS HAVEN'T BEEN USED IN *YEARS!*

THEY'RE ON NOW... GIVING OFF *A LOT* OF HEAT, TOO!

OOO-GAAA-LAAA-LAAA, OOO-GAAA-LAAA-LAA!

UHHH...YOU GUYS HEAR THAT?!

DISSEMBLE NO MORE! I ADMIT THE DEED!
TEAR UP THE PLANKS! HERE! IT IS THE ***BEATING*** OF HIS ***HIDEOUS HEART!***

NO, IT SOUNDS LIKE ***CHANTING!***
SNIFF! SNIFF!

GOOD BOY, CHAD! SNIFF IT OUT!

OOO-GAAA-LAAA-LAA, OOO-GAAA-LAAA-LAA!

ARF! ARF!

THERE'S NOTHING HERE! WEIRD...

!

GASP!

YOU'VE GOT A
PAL IN THE
PRINCIPAL'S
OFFICE!

MWAHAHAHA!

Chapter 3
THAT'S KINDA WEIRD

VROOOOOM!

TOY & HOBBY SHOP
NEXT STOP: FUNERAL, CLOWNS.

POOF!

AT THE FUNERAL HOME...
LORD BOOM BOOM BAGGY BRITCHES WAS A CLOWN'S CLOWN.
WE ALL HAVE BIG, FLOPPY SHOES TO FILL!
LORD BOOM BOOM'S HORN WOULD NOW LIKE TO SAY A FEW WORDS!

H K!
H K!

AT THIS TIME, YOU MAY PAY YOUR RESPECTS.

SOB!
SPLAT!

SOB!
SPRITZZ!

Q EAK!
SOB!

HONK!
WAAAAHH!

SOB!

TOY & HOBBY
SHOP

TOY & HOBBY
SHOP
QUEAK
QUEAK

QUEAK
QUEAK

MY MAKEUP... IT RUNS!

C-CAN'T SEE!

AHHHHHH!

WHAMMM!

FSSSSSS!

BOING!
CLANK!
CRASH!

BOING!
OOOF!

GROAN!

HMMM.

DING!
DONG!

AHHHHH!

AHHHHHHH!

WHAT DO YOU THINK YOU'RE DOING *SCARING* MY *BABY?!* WE'RE CALLING THE POLICE!

WHAT? NO, YOU DON'T UNDERSTAND! MY CAR!

BRUTUS, *KILL!*

WOOF!
WOOF!
WOOF!
YAAH!

SPLURCH!

AHHHHHHHHH!

AAAAH!

BACK AT P.S. 38...
I REALLY WANT TO KNOW WHERE ALL THAT NOISE IS COMING FROM! IT COULD JUST BE THE PIPES, RIGHT?

I MEAN, THIS PLACE IS PRETTY OLD...STUFF RATTLES AND CREAKS AND UHH...

OOOOOOOOOOOOOO!

AHHHHHH!

HI THERE!

WHAM!

CHAD?
Y-YOU
OKAY?

GULP!

YOU'VE GOT A
PAL IN THE
PRINCIPAL'S
OFFICE!

AHHHHHH!

GINA! I THOUGHT SO!

MWAHAHAHA! YOU SHOULD HAVE SEEN THE LOOKS ON YOUR FACES!

YOUR FEAR MAKES ME FEEL SO ALIVE!

BEAT IT, GINA! WE'VE GOT STUFF TO DO, AND YOU'RE IN OUR WAY!

NOT A CHANCE, NATE!
I'M STAYING RIGHT HERE TO KEEP AN EYE ON YOU... AND MAKE YOUR SILLY MACHINATIONS ALL COME TO A SCREECHING HALT!

MACHIN-A WHAT? LOOK, I DON'T KNOW WHAT THAT MEANS, BUT I DON'T CARE!
WHATEVER, NATE!
WHATEVER, GINA!

SNIFF! MMMMMM! I SMELL THE BEGUILING AROMA OF MYSTERY MEAT!

I'M GOING TO THE CAFETERIA!

OH! THAT'S A GOOD IDEA, CHAD. WE CAN DECORATE THE CAFETERIA, JUST TO BE SAFE!

GRUNT!

⋟SNIFF!⋞

⋟SNIFF!⋞

WHUMP!

WELL, HELLO, HOW ARE YOU?

I REALLY LIKE YOUR–

AHHHHHHH!
CRRRSH!

CHAD? *CHAD?!*

I KNEW IT! IT'S ALL CONNECTED!
THIS IS JUST LIKE THE LEGEND OF THE HORRIBLE COVEN OF MAN-WITCHES!

IT ALL STARTS WITH DISAPPEARING KIDS!!!

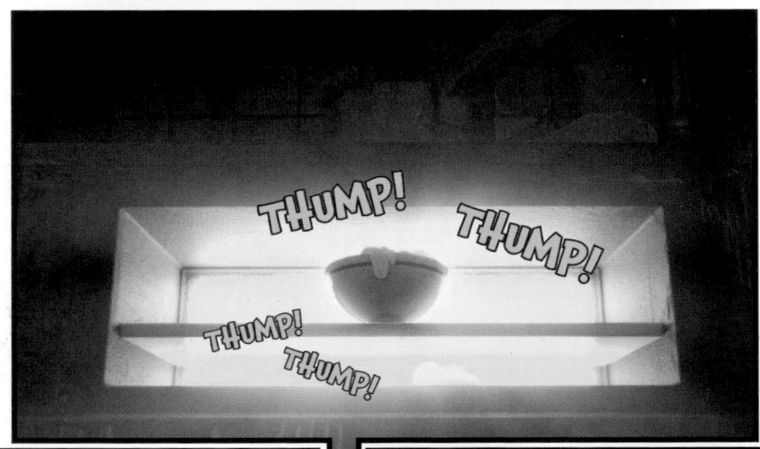
THUMP!
THUMP!
THUMP!
THUMP!

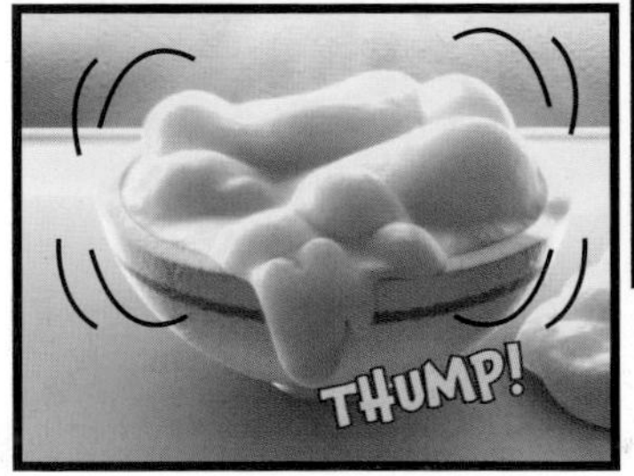
THUMP!

HUH?

AHHHHHHHH!

IS THAT...
IS THAT...
BLOOD?!

AHHHHHH!

HURRY, BAR THE DOOR!

HUH?

WHO'S THAT?

Chapter 4
IT'S NOT POSSIBLE!
YOU'VE HIRED SOMEBODY TO RUN AROUND IN A ***COSTUME?***
NO! I DIDN'T DO THAT, ***I SWEAR IT!***

RIIIIIGHT...

WHOEVER YOU ARE, I'M GOING TO STOP YOU FROM HELPING NATE!

HE WILL ***NOT*** GET OUT OF ANY TESTS!

I'VE GOT YOU NOW, NATE'S CO-CONSPIRATOR!

THERE'S NO ONE THERE!

I DON'T GET IT! IT'S NOT POSSIBLE...

AHHHHHH!

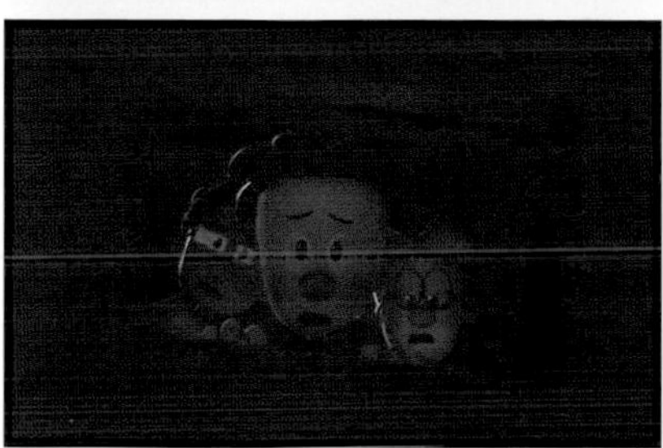

AHHHHHHHHHH!

HURRY, LET'S GET OUT OF HERE!
OH! OH, NO! OH, NO! THE ALARM'S BEEN SET!

IF WE TRIGGER THE ALARM, WE'LL GET EXPELLED!

GASP! WE'RE TRAPPED!

WAIT! LOOK! TEDDY IS ALREADY OUTSIDE!

WITHOUT TRIGGERING THE ALARM!
HOW DOES HE ALWAYS DO THAT?! AND HOW ARE WE GOING TO GET OUT?

DON'T GIVE UP HOPE, BOYS! I KNOW **EXACTLY** HOW TO DISARM THIS ALARM!
YOU DO?
HOW? AND... WHY?

THIS ALARM IS JUST LIKE THE SYSTEM I PRACTICED ON FOR MY ROLE AS...**DIAMOND SAL**, PROFESSIONAL SAFE-CRACKER, AND FORMER NAVY SEAL WRONGED BY THE GOVERNMENT SHE LOVED!

IT WAS A VERY COMPLEX PART. NOW **SILENCE!** I NEED A MINUTE TO GET BACK INTO CHARACTER SO I CAN CRACK THE CODE.

HANG ON...I THINK THERE'S SOMETHING WRONG WITH ME.
I THINK MY CONSCIENCE IS TELLING ME TO GO BACK AND SAVE GINA!
WHAT?! THAT'S CRAZY!

YEAH, YOU'RE RIGHT, LET'S GET THE HECK OUT OF HERE!
WAIT! I JUST REMEMBERED **CHAD!**

OH, YEAH... CHAD.

GUYS, WE CAN'T LET THEM GET EATEN!
WE DON'T ***KNOW*** THEY'RE BEING EATEN.

OM NOM NOM!
OM NOM NOM!

THAT IS CLEARLY WHAT CHAD AND GINA BEING EATEN SOUNDS LIKE!

I'M GOING TO GO SAVE THEM!
WE'LL GO WITH YOU, NATE!
WE WILL?
WE WILL.

NO...I WANT YOU TO GO ON WITHOUT ME! TELL MY STORY! TELL EVERYONE WHAT HAPPENED HERE!

AND PUT A NICE SOUNDTRACK UNDERNEATH WITH CRESCENDOING VIOLINS, MAYBE AN OBOE OR TWO!

ALL RIGHT, HERE GOES NOTHING!
⋽GULP!⋲

RISE! RISE!

BRING FORTH THE BLOB!

BLOB!...BLOB!...
BLOB!...BLOB!...

BLOB!...
BLOB!...
BLOB!...
BLOB!...

OH, THIS IS SO NOT GOOD...

MEANWHILE...
CLICK!

DIAMOND SAL, SHE'S THE GAL, A TOTAL WAIF, WHO CAN CRACK ANY SAFE...OR OPEN A DOOR!

WHATEVER, DIAMOND SAL. LET'S JUST GET OUT OF HERE!

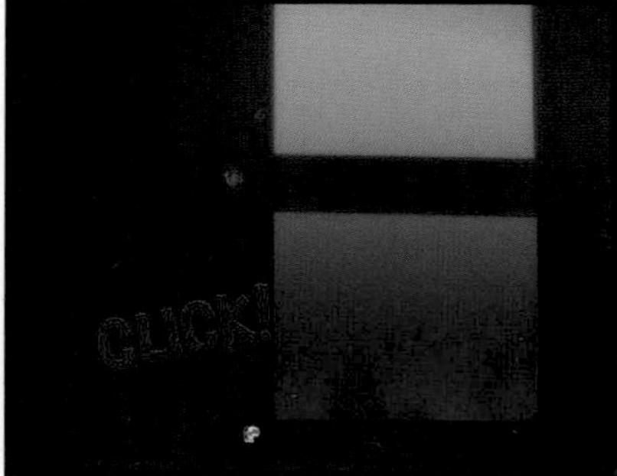
CLICK!

ELSEWHERE...
HELLO? CAN YOU HELP ME?
HUH?

I JUST NEED A HAND—
AHHHHHH!

WAIT, DON'T RUN AWAY! I NEED HELP!

AWOOOAWOO!
THAT'S A POLICE SIREN!

HELLO? HELLO! I'M DOWN HERE!

VERY FUNNY.
COME ON, BOZO, YOU'RE COMING WITH US!

HEY JOE, SOMEBODY TRIGGERED THE ALARM AT THE MIDDLE SCHOOL!
OH, IT'S JUST P.S. 38...NOT LIKE IT'S AT JEFFERSON OR SOMEWHERE ***IMPORTANT!***
BETTER TAKE A LOOK ANYWAY.

ALL RIGHT, YOU STAY HERE, CLOWN. WE'LL BE RIGHT BACK.

BACK AT P.S. 38...
RISE! RISE! RISE! RISE!
WOOOHOOOO!

OH, NO! THEY'RE GOING TO FEED GINA AND CHAD TO THAT HORRIBLE BLOB!

RISE! *RISE!*

RISE! RISE! RISE! RISE!

NOOOOO! I WON'T LET YOU EAT THEM!

I'M GOING IN!

AHHHHHH!

SPLAT!

CHARGE!

WHAM!

WHAT ARE YOU *DOING*, YOU DOORKNOB?!
I'M TRYING TO SAVE YOU AND CHAD FROM THE MAN-WITCHES!

GROAN!

MR. ROSA?

WE'RE NOT WITCHES OF *ANY* KIND!

WAIT, WHAT? WHAT'S GOING ON!? PRINCIPAL NICHOLS? COACH JOHN?

MR. GALVIN? I DON'T GET IT.

AND WHAT'S WITH ALL THE *CREEPY DOUGH* EVERYWHERE?

WE'RE PRACTICING TO WIN THE BIG MIDDLE SCHOOL BAKING COMPETITION!

WE'VE CREATED A SPECIAL *TRIPLE-DECKER DEEP-DISH PIE CAKE!*

IT'S A **PIZZA**, A **PIE**, AND A **CAKE**. GET IT?

BUT WHY ARE YOU WEARING THOSE CREEPY ROBES AND HOODS?

TO KEEP OUR CLOTHES CLEAN WHILE WE WERE BAKING! DO YOU KNOW HOW **HARD** IT IS TO GET PEPPERONI STAINS OUT OF A PAIR OF **KHAKIS?**

WE DISCOVERED THAT THE OLD BOILER WAS THE PERFECT "BRICK OVEN" TO WORK ON OUR SPECIAL PIZZA FOR THE COMPETITION. KISMET!

IT'S A **PIZZA**, A **PIE**, AND A **CAKE. GET IT?!** YOU **GET IT?!**
THEY GET IT, JOHN. THEY'RE HIP, HAPPENING KIDS. BE QUIET NOW.

THAT EXPLAINS THE **BIG BLOBBY MONSTER!** YOU WERE JUST FEEDING A YEAST MIXTURE IN ORDER FOR THE DOUGH TO RISE!

EXACTLY!

THUMP!
THUMP!
"WHICH ALSO EXPLAINS THE THUMPING GHOST BOWL IN THE OVEN IN THE CAFETERIA...
"...AND THE BLOODY HANDPRINT WAS ACTUALLY JUST MARINARA PIZZA SAUCE!"

OM NOM NOM

AND THAT'S THE WEIRD EATING SOUND WE HEARD EARLIER. HUH. WHOA, OKAY, I SEE WHAT YOU DID WRONG HERE.

YOU GOT THE RATIO ALL WRONG FOR THE AMOUNTS OF YEAST, SUGAR, AND FLOUR. LET'S JUST SEE HERE...DO A LITTLE BIT OF THIS, STIR THIS...

YEAH, I THINK YOU'LL FIND **THIS** IS A BETTER MIX FOR YOUR DOUGH.

NATE WRIGHT, HAVE YOU REALLY BEEN ***PAYING ATTENTION*** IN MY CHEMISTRY CLASS?
PFFTT... UMM, NO...

BUT YOU'VE ACTUALLY ***LEARNED*** ABOUT CHEMISTRY!

LOOK, I JUST KNOW ABOUT PIZZA AND BAKING, I GUESS.

BAKING ***IS*** CHEMISTRY!

WHOA! MIND BLOWN!

CRASH!

DAD?!
I'M HERE TO SAVE YOU, SON...

I HEARD ABOUT THE **WITCHES** AND THANK **HEAVENS** YOU'RE OKAY AND I WAS ON MY WAY HOME BECAUSE ALL I REALLY WANTED TO DO WAS JUST BE A **GOOD CLOWN** FOR MY FRIEND. BUT WAS I?

I SCARED A **CHILD!** WALLOWED IN **SEWAGE!** HOW DOES **THAT** HONOR THE MEMORY OF A FALLEN CLOWN? **WAHHHHH!**

WHAT'S GOING ON HERE?

YOU CAN'T TAKE ME AGAIN!

ZIP!

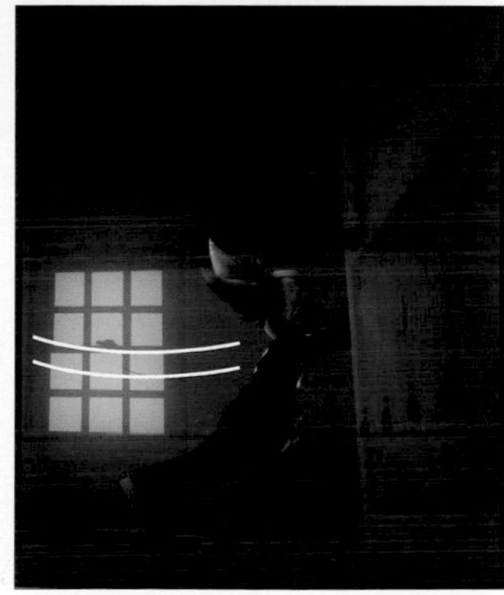

AHHH!!!
POP!
POP!

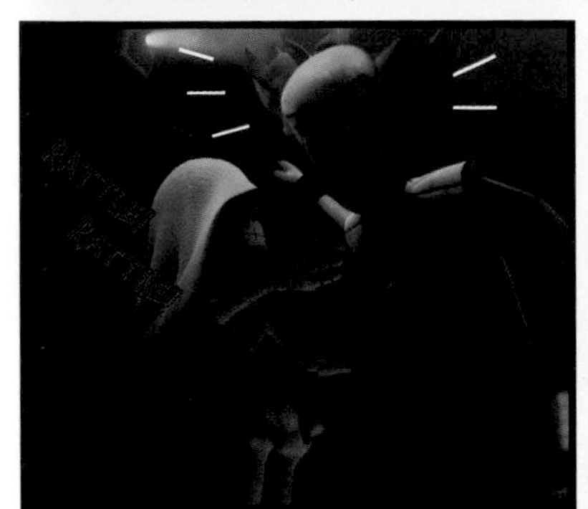

AHHH!!!

HELLLP!

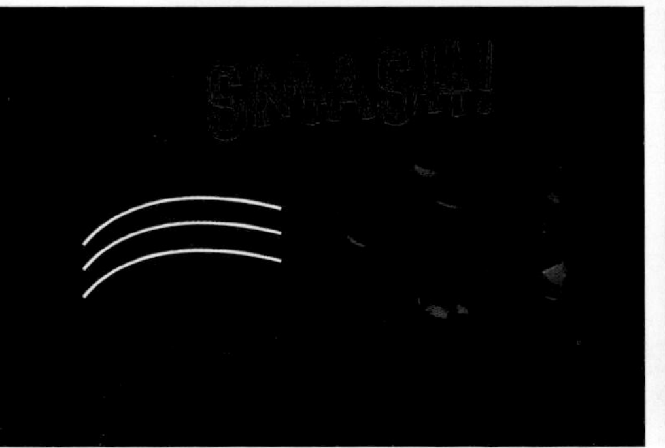
SMASH!

AHHH!!!

"OH YEAH, IT'S A BEAUTIFUL DAY. MR. GALVIN ACTUALLY CANCELED CLASS BECAUSE HE WAS SO TIRED FROM BEING UP ALL NIGHT."
PS38

SO, I'VE GOTTEN MYSELF AND ALL MY FRIENDS OUT OF THAT ***HORRIBLE*** CHEMISTRY TEST! HA HA! YEP! IT PROMISES TO BE THE BEST DAY ***EVER***...

ALL RIGHT, CLASS. WELCOME TO THE ***SURPRISE*** MIDTERM SOCIAL STUDIES TEST!

GUESS THERE REALLY ***ARE*** WITCHES IN THIS SCHOOL.

MWAHAHAHA!

THE SCHOOL'S KIND OF CREEPY AT NIGHT.
EXACTLY!

AND **OUR** JOB IS TO MAKE IT EVEN CREEPIER!
SHH! WHAT'S THAT?
BEEYOWLLL

BEEYOWLLLLL
IT'S EITHER A GHOSTLY COVEN OF MAN-WITCHES...

...OR NOT.
CHAD?
SORRY, GUYS! MAJOR GAS BUBBLE!
BEEYOWLLLLL

The Curse of the Applewhites

Chapter 1
GYM-ITIS
'SCUSE ME! BIG DAY TODAY!

WE'RE STARTING WINTER SPORTS IN GYM CLASS...

...AND IF I DON'T GET THERE ON TIME...

OOF!

...I WON'T GET TO SIGN UP FOR ICE HOCKEY!

SQUEEZING THROUGH!

ALSO, I'M TOTALLY COUNTING ON IT TO SAVE MY GRADE!

I GOTTA MAKE SURE I GET ICE HOCKEY, BECAUSE OTHERWISE I'LL HAVE TO DO—

TWWWWTTT!

GULP!

FIGURE SKATING!

ALL RIGHT, MAGGOTS, **GET AFTER IT!**

YOU WANT US TO SKATE? ON ***THAT?***

USE YOUR IMAGINATION, SCRUB! THIS IS A FROSTED WINTER WONDERLAND! AN OLYMPIC ICE RINK!

HISSSS!
GRRR!

OOH, I THINK I SEE IT! LIKE THE NORTH POLE...

...BUT IF SANTA *HATED* US.

AHHH!

NOW GET OUT THERE AND *SKATE!*

AHHH!

HO-HO-***NO!*** HOW DID ***ALL*** OF MY FRIENDS GET ICE HOCKEY EXCEPT FOR ME?!

FWIP!

FWIP!

GROAN! ALL RIGHT, REAL TALK?

"MY SISTER ELLEN **LOVES** TO TORTURE ME, AND FIGURE SKATING IS HER ***WEAPON OF NATE DESTRUCTION!***
WHO-**AAAH!**

SCHNICK!

WOOO!
WHACK!

"YOU'D HATE FIGURE SKATING WITH THE WHITE-HOT INTENSITY OF A THOUSAND SUNS, TOO, IF YOU WENT THROUGH WHAT ***I*** HAVE."
PUSH!

WHOAAA!

FWIP!
FWIP!
FWIP!
FWIP!

AHHHH!
SPLSHHH!

NOW, BACK TO OUR STORY.

FRONT AND CENTER, JUNIOR! GET OVER HERE! ***NOW!!***

GROAN!

HERE GOES NOTHING.

SIGH!

LATER.
HEY, CHAMP! HOW YA FEELIN'?

COUGH! TERRIBLE. I THINK I'LL BE OUT FOR THE WHOLE SCHOOL YEAR, DAD.

I THINK I KNOW WHAT'S GOING ON HERE. YOU'VE GOT A BAD CASE OF *GYM-ITIS.*

I USED TO GET IT ALL THE TIME DUE TO MY COMPLETE LACK OF PROPER MUSCLE FORMATION.

SIGH! IT'S A WONDER I CAN EVEN FEED MYSELF.

DAD, CAN YOU PLEASE JUST EXCUSE ME FROM GYM? I HAVEN'T ASKED YOU FOR *ANYTHING* LATELY!

THAT'S NOT QUITE TRUE...

DAD, CAN I HAVE YOUR WAFFLES?
ZIP!

DAD, CAN I HAVE THE COMICS SECTION?
NAB!

HEY, DAD, CAN I HAVE THIS CHAINSAW?

PLEEEAASE! PLEASE GET ME OUT OF GYM CLASS!

TIME
DISRUPTORS

DON'T LET HIM GET TO YOU, MARTY. BE STRONG! YOU HAVE TO TELL HIM NO.

NUH...

NUH...

NURRRRRRR...

SO...
DIZZY...

UH,
DAD?
ZIP!

WELL, THAT WASN'T A "NO." AND A "NOT NO" EQUALS A ***"YES!"***

HOW CAN I SAY ***NO*** TO HIM WITHOUT CRUSHING HIS SPIRIT?!
DO
NOT

THE NEXT DAY: ATTEMPT ONE.
WHAT IN TARNATION?!

HELLO, COACH JOHN. AS YOU CAN SEE, I'VE HAD A LITTLE ACCIDENT. SHAME I WON'T BE ABLE TO FIGURE SKATE TODAY!

NICE CAST. WHAT DID YOU USE? TWO-PLY?
HEH HEH! UH...IT'S A MIRACLE! I AM CURED.

BE RIGHT BACK!
ZIP!

ATTEMPT TWO.
MY **FEAR THE MOLLUSK** ALBUM GOT DISCOVERED BY THE **HOTTEST** K-POP BAND IN THE GAME!

AS A K-POP FAN MYSELF, I'M **HIGHLY** SKEPTICAL.

ATTEMPT THREE.
HEY HEY! HO HO! THESE ICE SKATES HAVE GOT TO GO!

I WILL BE SITTING OUT GYM CLASS AS A FORM OF PROTEST AGAINST CHILD HUMILIATION IN THIS COUNTRY.

GRAB!

IF YOU THINK FIGURE SKATING IS HUMILIATING, TRY *REPEATING* SIXTH GRADE GYM!

GO LACE UP, PORCUPINE HEAD!

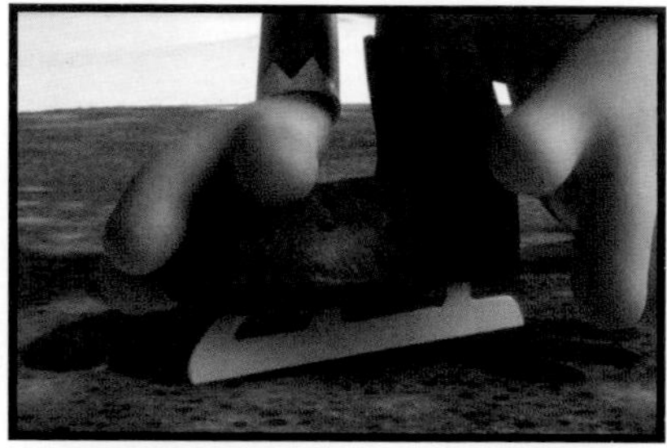

"LACE UP, PORCUPINE HEAD!"

AT LEAST *I* DON'T WEAR A TOUPÉE THAT LOOKS LIKE A DEAD MUSKRAT!
HEY, NATE! HOW'S IT GOIN'?

HOW'S IT GOIN'? ***HOW'S IT GOIN'?*** DEE DEE, IF YOU DIDN'T NOTICE, I HAVE TO ***FIGURE SKATE!***

AND...?

WELL FOR STARTERS, BECAUSE OF ELLEN, I'VE SWORN A BLOOD OATH TO HATE FIGURE SKATING!
NOT TO MENTION I AM GOING TO ***TOTALLY*** EMBARRASS MYSELF!
WHEN I DANCE I LOOK LIKE...

A TOTAL DORK? MAYBE YOU CAN FIND A ***PARTNER*** TO TAKE THE PRESSURE OFF! AT ACTING CAMP, WHEN I DID "LASSIE, I'M GASSY," MY TWO-PERSON PLAY...

...CORRECTION, IT WAS ONE PERSON, ONE DOG, BUT YOU GET THE IDEA...

STOP! YOU'VE SAID SOMETHING I'VE CHOSEN TO PAY ATTENTION TO!

PARTNER, PARTNER, PARTNER...I NEED A...

EH, NO, DON'T HAVE A DEATH WISH.

♫ ♪
HMM!

HEY CHAD!

WHAT ARE YOU DOING UP THERE?

MAKING PAPER SNOWFLAKES.

GRRR!

CRUMPLE!

SOOOOOO, C-DOG, C-MEISTER, CHAD-O-RAMA, OL' BUDDY...I WAS THINKING...

SORRY, NATE, BUT MY FRECKLES ARE TINGLING... WHICH MEANS YOU'RE ABOUT TO ASK ME TO BE YOUR FIGURE SKATING PARTNER AND I MUST RESPECTFULLY DECLINE!

WHAT ABOUT ***KIM?*** SHE DOESN'T HAVE A PARTNER! AND SHE'S AS STRONG AS A BOX!

UM, I DON'T THINK A ***BOX*** IS VERY STRONG, CHAD.

BOX. HALF BEAR, HALF OX.

HEY. LET'S SKATE.

YEOW!

AHHH!

FWIP!

WOOSH!

KRRRKRKR!

MMMM. A SOUVENIR.

Chapter 2
HOW TO TRAIN YOUR NATE
SORRY TO TAKE UP YOUR TIME. I DIDN'T KNOW WHERE ELSE TO TURN.

YOU WERE WISE TO COME TO US.

LET ME GUESS: NATE ASKED YOU TO GET HIM OUT OF GYM CLASS, AND YOU CAN'T SAY NO.
THAT'S RIGHT! HOW DID YOU KNOW?

SIGH. THIS HAS BEEN GOING ON FOR YEARS, MR. WRIGHT.

HEY, DAD, I'M GONNA HAVE CHEESY SNACKS FOR DINNER...

...THAT'S COOL RIGHT?

N–

SIGH.

HEY! I MADE A ZIP LINE OUT OF ELLEN'S HAIR!

SHE SHEDS MORE THAN SPITSY! SOUND GOOD TO YOU?

N......

YAHOO!

HAHAHA!

CRASH!!

KAW!
HEY, HEY, HEY! I JUST ADOPTED THE ENTIRE ANIMAL SHELTER!
OINK!
OINK!
KAW!

WHOA, WHOA! THE LEMURS ARE BITING MY ANKLES! CAN WE KEEP THEM ALL, DAD?!
KAW!
KAW!

NNNUUUUUU–

≥SIGH.≤
OINK!
OINK!

YOU KIDS ARE ***RIGHT!*** I'VE CREATED A ***MONSTER!*** ≥SOB!≤

SOB!

THERE, THERE, MARTIN. IT'S NOT TOO LATE.

WE'VE GOT THE ***PERFECT*** THREE-STEP PLAN TO MAKE NATE RESPECT YOU AS AN AUTHORITY FIGURE. IT IS FOOLPROOF, IF I SAY SO MYSELF!

I CAN'T THANK YOU ENOUGH, CHILDREN!

WHY DID IT HAVE TO BE FIGURE SKATING? I'M GONNA NEED A MIRACLE TO GET OUT OF THIS!

LA DI DA DI DA DI DAAA...
HIDDEN POND PARK
GASP!
YOU HEARING THAT TOO?

LA DI DA!
FWIP!

MIRACLE, HERE I COME!

HEY, CHAD!
CRASH!
OOF!

NATE! WHAT ARE YOU DOING HERE? NO ONE WAS SUPPOSED TO KNOW ABOUT THIS!

AWWW, WHAT DO YOU MEAN, BUDDY? YOU'RE THE ANSWER TO ALL MY HOPES AND DREAMS!

IT'S NOT ***SAFE*** FOR YOU TO SEE ME!

WHAT JUST HAPPENED?

AS NATE'S MOST ENABLING-EST FRIEND, ALLOW ME TO INTRODUCE STEP 1 IN YOUR COURSE: ***MISCHIEF MANAGEMENT!***
HOW TO TRAIN your Nate

I WILL BE TEACHING YOU HOW TO RECOGNIZE THE SEEDLINGS OF MISCHIEF IN NATE BEFORE THEY BLOSSOM INTO A FULL-GROWN, CARNIVOROUS PLANT THAT WILL INEVITABLY DESTROY US ALL!
STEP 1:
MISCHIEF
Management

OBSERVE. THE CRAZY GLEAM NATE GETS IN HIS EYE AS HE'S CONJURING UP A WILD IDEA.

HEY! I RECOGNIZE THAT LOOK!
OF COURSE YOU DO, NATE'S DAD!
OH, PLEASE... CALL ME MARTIN.

NOW THESE ARE SOME OF THE THINGS NATE SAYS BEFORE HE'S ABOUT TO COMMIT *UNA LOCURA*.
ANY ONE OF THESE SHOULD PUT YOU ON HIGH ALERT.
HiGH ALERT PHRASES

"I have an idea!"

"I got this."

"What happens if I push THIS button?"

"Do you dare me to eat this?"

AND LAST BUT NOT LEAST...
"Can 11 year olds get arrested for____?"

Chapter 3
THE CURSE OF THE APPLEWHITES

HEY, CHAD. LOOK, I KNOW THIS IS A LITTLE AWKWARD, BUT CAN WE TALK ABOUT WHAT HAPPENED YESTERDAY ON THE POND?

W-UH—SIGH. WE HAVE TO BE QUICK.

MY MOM AND GRANDMA ARE OUT MILKING THE CATS, BUT THEY'LL BE BACK ANY MINUTE.

HOLD UP. YOU CAN *MILK* A *CAT?*

OH, YEAH! IT'S TRICKY, BUT TOTALLY WORTH IT. CAT ICE CREAM IS ***DELICIOUS!***
GAG!

SLURP!
EW!

BURRRP!

SORRY, NATE. THAT WAS SO RUDE OF ME. WOULD YOU LIKE A GLASS?

CHAD, WHY ARE YOU BEING SO STRANGE?

Whisk
Sparkles

I MEAN, STRANGER THAN USUAL. AND WHY IS THE WORD "ICE" CROSSED OUT ON YOUR ICE MAKER?

slow water
Maker

SHHH! N-N-N-NO! WE DON'T SAY THAT WORD IN THIS HOUSE!

WHAT WORD? ***ICE?***
DUDE, ARE YOUR MOM AND GRANDMA VIGILANTE OUTLAWS? BECAUSE THAT WOULD BE ***AWESOME!***

SLURP!

NO MORE SECRETS.

BURP!

MEOW!

THEY DON'T KNOW I KNOW WHERE THIS IS.

CRACK!

GRUNT!

BLURG!

ROWR!

KLIK!

WHOA!

CHAD, WHO ARE ALL THOSE PICTURES OF?

WELL, THIS IS POP POP APPLEWHITE, AND THIS IS GREAT POP POP APPLEWHITE, AND THIS, OF COURSE, IS GREAT GREAT POP POP APPLEWHITE...

OKAY, Y'KNOW WHAT? GENUINELY SORRY I ASKED.

NATE, I THINK IT'S ABOUT TIME THAT I TELL YOU THE TALE OF ***"THE CURSE OF THE APPLEWHITES."***

Cursed

IN THE OLD COUNTRY, THE APPLEWHITES... OR, AS THEY PRONOUNCED IT BACK THEN, THE PFLURGENSTUMPS...WERE EXPERT FIGURE SKATERS, BELOVED BY ALL.
The Applewhites

"PEOPLE CAME FROM FAR AND WIDE TO SEE THEM SKATE.

"BUT WHEN BOGUS SANTA CLAUSES STARTED OFFERING HALF-PRICE SLEIGH RIDES...

"...THE APPLEWHITES' POPULARITY STARTED TO WITHER AND DIE.
½ Price

KRA-KOOOOOW!

"THAT'S WHEN MY GREAT GREAT GREAT GREAT POP POP WENT SEARCHING FOR THE ALL-POWERFUL SEQUINIA...

"SEQUINIA SHOWED HIM THE ***RUSTY BUZZSAW,*** A MOVE SO COMPLEX THAT IT WOULD, ONCE MASTERED, MAKE OUR FAMILY THE GREATEST FIGURE SKATERS OF ALL TIME.

"BUT IT WAS A TRAP! SEQUINIA KNEW THAT PERFORMING THE RUSTY BUZZSAW IS ALMOST IMPOSSIBLE!

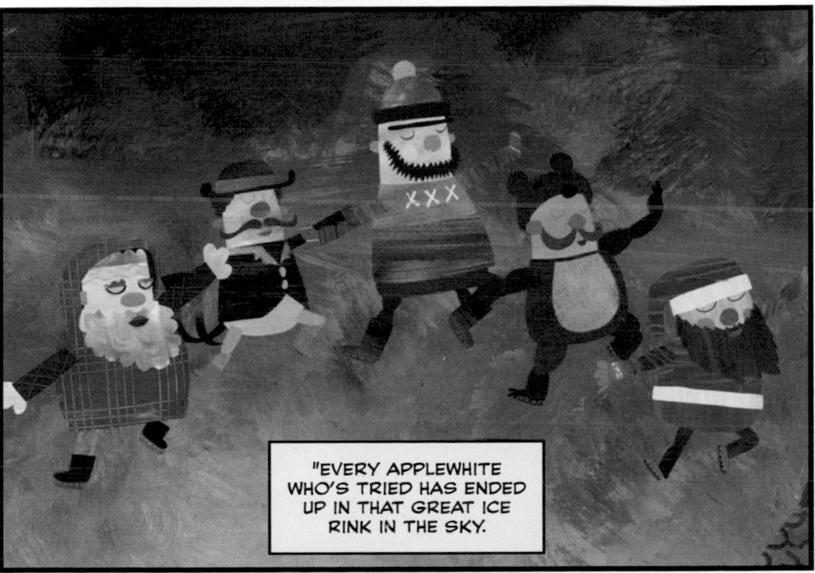
"EVERY APPLEWHITE WHO'S TRIED HAS ENDED UP IN THAT GREAT ICE RINK IN THE SKY.

"AND THAT'S HOW THE MOVE MEANT TO BRING MY FAMILY FAME...INSTEAD BECAME A ***CURSE!***"
RIP
RIP
RIP
RIP
RIP
RIP
RIP

FIGURE SKATING HAS BEEN FORBIDDEN IN THE APPLEWHITE FAMILY EVER SINCE!

CHAD, MY BOY, YOU'RE IN LUCK!

NATE WRIGHT IS GOING TO GRACIOUSLY AND SELFLESSLY HELP YOU BREAK THAT CURSE!
...WHILE YOU HELP ME OVERCOME MY DEEP TRAUMA AROUND FIGURE SKATING SO I DON'T EMBARRASS MYSELF IN FRONT OF THE ENTIRE SCHOOL!
AND DID I MENTION I MADE A BLOOD OATH?

YOU DID.
OKAY.

OKAY? WAIT, THAT'S IT? AFTER ALL THAT?
I'M EASY!

OKAY, CHAD...SHOW ME SOME OF THAT APPLEWHITE MAGIC!

I HEARD YOU FOUND ANOTHER PARTNER, DOES HE ICE SKATE BETTER THAN I CAN?

I SAW IT WITH MY OWN EYES...

...I FELL TO THE GROUND...
...IS IT BECAUSE I TURNED YOU INTO A POPSICLE?

I GUESS THAT MAY HAVE BEEN A LITTLE MUCH...

IS THAT WHAT MADE YOU GIVE UP ON OUR LOVE?

I'M IN THE BUSHES WATCHING YOU TWO SKATE!

I'M HERE JUST THROUGH THOSE LEAVES...

...CAN YOU NOT FEEL ME?
OH NO NO...

I AM STARING MY HARDEST BUT I'M NOT THE ONE YOU'RE SKATING WITH...

OOH NO NO NO NO NO...

I'M SKATING BY MYSELF, ALL ALONE... *SIGH*

YEAH!
HA! HA!

CHAD, WE'VE BEEN AT THIS FOR **HOURS.**
MAYBE IT'S TIME WE ATTEMPT... THE ***RUSTY BUZZSAW!***
YEAH, I MEAN WHY NOT? I'VE HAD A FULL LIFE!

READY?
READY!

GRUNT!
YAAH!

WHAM!

WHAT DO YOU THINK YOU'RE DOING!

MOM! GRAM! HOW DID YOU FIND ME?!

WE WERE OUT MILKING SPARKLES WHEN GRAM PICKED UP YOUR SCENT.

FEMALE APPLEWHITES HAVE POWERFUL SNIFFERS! IT'S HOW WE SURVIVED SO LONG IN THE OLD COUNTRY!
THIS ISN'T WHAT IT LOOKS LIKE!

IT LOOKS LIKE MY SON
IS ENGAGED IN FORBIDDEN
MOONLIGHT ICE SKATING WITH
HIS BEST FRIEND!

WELL, IT'S
EXACTLY WHAT
IT LOOKS LIKE.

YOU ARE
GROUNDED! INDEFINITELY!
YOU WILL NEVER
ICE SKATE OR SEE THAT
FOUL-SMELLING WRIGHT
BOY EVER AGAIN!

WHIMPER.

SNIFF
SNIFF I
SMELL?

MEANWHILE...

WELCOME TO *STEP 2: HOMEWORK!*
STEP 2

STEP 2
IT'S IMPORTANT FOR NATE TO ACTUALLY GET HIS HOMEWORK DONE. NOT ONLY WILL HE GET BETTER GRADES, BUT THE ACADEMIC EFFORT WILL SHARPEN HIS BRAIN!

HA!
HA!
HA!
HA!
HA!
STEP 2

MARTIN, WELCOME TO THE LAST STEP OF YOUR TRAINING. ***STEP 3: REVERSE IMPROV.***
ARE YOU FAMILIAR WITH THE CONCEPT OF "YES AND..."?

YES, AND–

SPLLLSH!

NO AND! ALL RIGHT. YOU'RE NOT GETTING IT.
SO ALL YOU HAVE TO DO IS SAY "NO AND..." TO OUR CRAZY ASKS...

...SO WHEN NATE COMES TO YOU WITH A NUTSO IDEA, YOU'RE READY TO SAY ***"NO."***

HEY, MR. WRIGHT! I MEAN, DAD!
COOL IF I SKIP SCHOOL FOR THE DAY TO GO SKATEBOARDING?

I FEEL DIRTY EVEN SAYING THAT.
SURE THING, SON!

FFFST!

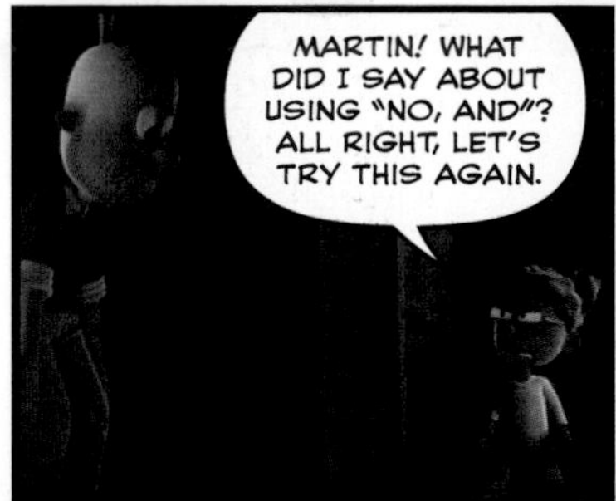
MARTIN! WHAT DID I SAY ABOUT USING "NO, AND"? ALL RIGHT, LET'S TRY THIS AGAIN.

AHEM. I'M GOING TO TRY BUNGEE JUMPING WITH A CORD MADE OF TOILET PAPER!

HMM. ARE WE TALKING PUBLIC RESTROOM TOILET PAPER OR EXTRA PLUSH?

I MEAN... NNNOOUUIIRRRRR... *SIGH.* YES.

I DON'T
THINK I
CAN DO
THIS!

MARTIN, WHAT'S WRONG?
OH, I DON'T KNOW, DEE DEE. I GUESS I JUST DON'T LIKE THE WORD "NO." YOU SEE, THE WORLD HAS TOLD ME "NO" SO MANY TIMES!
LIKE THE TIME I WANTED TO START A ROCK BAND OF MIMES, OR WEAR A TRASH CAN AS CLOTHES!

THE WORLD JUST WASN'T READY.
I DON'T THINK I HAVE IT IN ME TO SAY "NO" TO NATE!

THANKS FOR TRYING, ANYWAY.

POOR NATE'S DAD. HE DOESN'T STAND A CHANCE!

THE FINAL PERFORMANCE

ALL RIGHT, KIDS, HUDDLE UP AND LISTEN HERE.
HEY, COACH JOHN, WHERE'S CHAD?

HE'S DOING ***ALTERNATIVE*** GYM.

BUT THAT'S FOR THE ***SCARY*** KIDS!

GYM
Exercise your PATIENCE!
• •
FLAMING SPITBALLS? WHAT WILL THEY THINK OF NEXT!?
FOOOMM!

SHOOOSH!

PSSSST!

HEY, CHAD!

NATE! WHAT ARE YOU DOING HERE?!

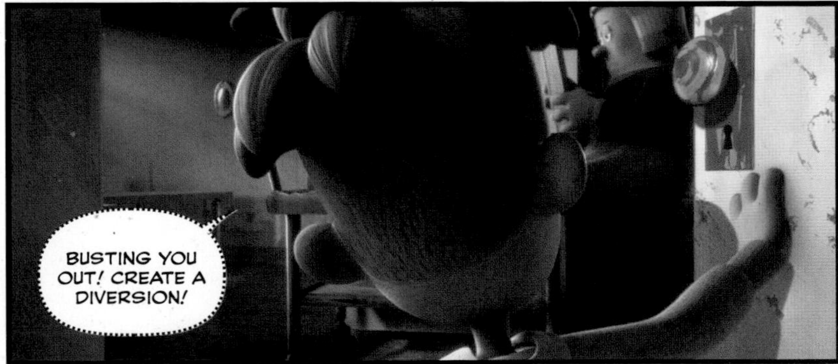
BUSTING YOU OUT! CREATE A DIVERSION!

I SAID, ***CREATE A DIVERSION.***

OKAY. HERE.

x²-6x+14
x+2) x³-4x²+2x-3
x³+2x²
-6x²+2x
-6x²-12x
14x-3
14x+28
-31

GRRR!

DIVERSION IS MATH, RIGHT?

I ALWAYS GOTTA DO EVERYTHING MYSELF!

TURKEY LEG!

ZING!

SPLAT!

GRRRR!

WHAM!

HEY, NICE WORK, PARTNER!

I DON'T KNOW IF WE SHOULD REALLY BE TALKING, NATE. Y'SEE, GRAM FORBID IT AND SHE'S A SCARY, ***SCARY LADY.***
THEY USED TO STICK HER IN FIELDS TO SCARE CROWS AWAY!

CHAD, ***FOCUS!*** I NEED YOUR HELP AND YOU NEED MINE!
IF WE WORK TOGETHER, WE CAN BREAK THIS CURSE AND PASS GYM CLASS!

YOU KNOW WHAT I HAVE TO SAY TO THAT, NATE?
RRIP!
WHOA, DO YOU ***ALWAYS*** WEAR THAT?

HEY NOW, LADIES AND GENTSICLES! IT'S TIME FOR OUR FIGURE SKATERS TO TAKE THE ICE! FIRST UP, KIM CRESSLY. GIVE IT UP!

C'MON NATE!

ER, THANK YOU, KIM, FOR THAT VERY CONFUSING AND SLIGHTLY ***CONCERNING*** PERFORMANCE.

THESE KIDS GET WEIRDER AND WEIRDER EVERY YEAR.

OKAY! NOW, LAST BUT NOT LEAST, NATE WRIGHT TO THE ICE, PLEASE!

NATE WRIGHT!

LET'S GO!

HEH HEH, I JUST LOVE FLUNKING KIDS IN GYM!

LAST CALL FOR NATE WRIGHT!

AH, *THERE* YOU ARE.
AND IT LOOKS LIKE HE BROUGHT A PARTNER! THESE CRAZY KIDS *LOVE* TO KEEP ME ON MY FROSTBITTEN TOES!

APPLEWHITE! WHAT ARE YOU DOING OUT OF YOUR PORTABLE?

CHAD, WHAT ARE YOU DOING?!

SOMETHING I SHOULD HAVE DONE A LONG TIME AGO!

BUT YOUR POP POP! AND HIS POP POP! AND HIS POP POP'S POP POP! AND–

LADIES, I'M GOING TO HAVE TO INSIST THAT YOU SIT DOWN. MMMKAY? BOOTIES DOWN, PLEASE. BOOTIES DOWN.

PARTNER?
PARTNER!

OOOH!

CLAP!
CLAP!
CLAP!
CLAP!

ARE THEY DOING... THE ***RUSTY BUZZSAW?***
THIS MOVE HAS KILLED MORE FIGURE SKATERS THAN SPANDEX POISONING!
CAN THEY DO THIS??

AHEM. COACH JOHN, PLEASE TELL ME THEY SIGNED A LIABILITY WAIVER.
ERR...

MARTIN, YOU CAN PUT A STOP TO THIS! JUST SAY **"NO"**! IT'S TOO DANGEROUS!

SOME TRULY HORRIBLE INJURIES COULD COME FROM THIS!

FROSTBITE. LIMBS SNAPPING LIKE TWIGS.

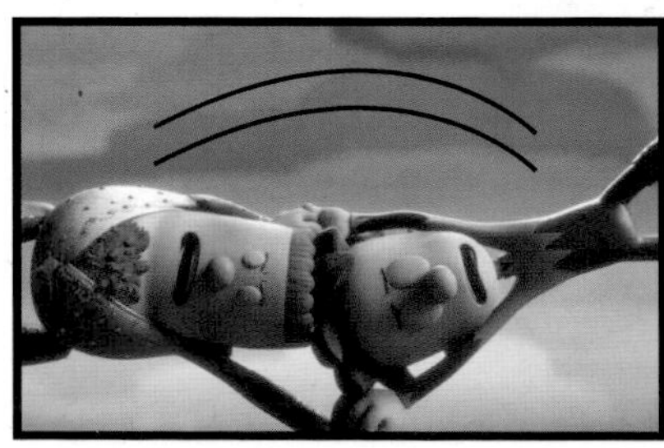

OH, NO!

AHHHH! WHAT WERE WE THINKING?!

N–

KKKKRSHH!

NATE'S DAD!
MARTIN!!!
MR. WRIGHT!

MY GOD, I DON'T THINK A SOUL HAS EVER SURVIVED THIS MOVE...
AHHHH!

GASP!

NOOOOOOOO!
FOOSH!

GRAB!

THOOM!

DAD, YOU **SAVED** US!

NO. NO.
NOOOO!
NO. NO. NO.
NO!!!!

YOU DID
IT, NATE'S
DAD!
YOU CAN
STOP
SAYING
"NO" NOW.
NO!
NOOOOO!!!!

SON, I WOULD
RATHER CRUSH YOUR
SPIRIT THAN HAVE YOU
CRUSH YOUR FACE
DOING SOMETHING
DANGEROUS.

BUT WHAT
ABOUT THE
CURSE?
WELL, TECHNICALLY, WE
COMPLETED THE MOVE.
MY DAD JUST HELPED US
STICK THE LANDING.

MOM, GRAM, THE
FAMILY CURSE IS BROKEN!

RATS! THOUGHT I HAD ANOTHER ONE!

AHHHH!

THE "B" IS FOR JUST **BARELY** PASSING, AND THE MINUS IS FOR THE HELP FROM DADDY.

B-

PASSED GYM, BROKE A CURSE! NOBODY BUT ***NATE WRIGHT*** COULDA PULLED THIS OFF!

WHO WANTS TO SKATE?

COACH JOHN! I'M HERE TO SIGN UP FOR ICE HOCKEY!
TOO LATE, SCRUB. ALL THE SPOTS ARE TAKEN.

YOU'LL DO FIGURE SKATING INSTEAD.
WHAT?

BUT I **HATE** FIGURE SKATING! AND ALL MY FRIENDS ARE PLAYING **HOCKEY**!

I SHALL SKATE WITH YOU, MY LOVE.
THIS JUST KEEPS GETTING WORSE.

'Til Death Do We Rock

Chapter 1
NEXT STOP: SUPERSTARDOM
Mollusk

LADIES AND GENTLEMEN, I GIVE YOU...**FEAR THE MOLLUSK!**

CAFETERIA MUSH, CAFETERIA MUSH, YOU'RE A STICKY MYSTERY TO ME THAT I LOVE TO EAT...

WHY I'D WANT TO EAT YOU I JUST DON'T UNDERSTAND...

OOOOOH OOOOOOH!
YOU'RE GOOEY AND HARD, SPICY AND BLAND...

TA-DA!

HOW'D I DO GUYS?! I DID GREAT, RIGHT?!
GROAN!
MY BRAIN HURTS!

YOU KNOW, THERE'S SOMETHING ABOUT BEING A LEAD SINGER IN A ROCK BAND THAT MAKES YOU FEEL INVINCIBLE!

MAYBE IT'S THE ACCESS TO ALL THE *HOT CLUBS...*
JOIN OUR SCIENCE CLUB!

MAYBE IT'S THE ENDLESS THRONG OF GROUPIES...
AYYY!
I GOT A PIECE OF NATE WRIGHT'S HAIR!
SNIP!

WHO'S NATE WRIGHT?
HOW DARE YOU!

OR *MAYBE* IT'S THE IRREFUTABLE FACT THAT THE GIRL I'VE BEEN CRUSHING ON SINCE THE FIRST GRADE WILL FINALLY HAVE TO NOTICE ME. ⋺SIGH!⋲ *JENNY.*

OH, JENNY, MY LOVE!
ARTUR!
⋺GROAN!⋲
YOUR EYES GLISTEN LIKE THE OIL IN STYLGRAVIAN LAKE!

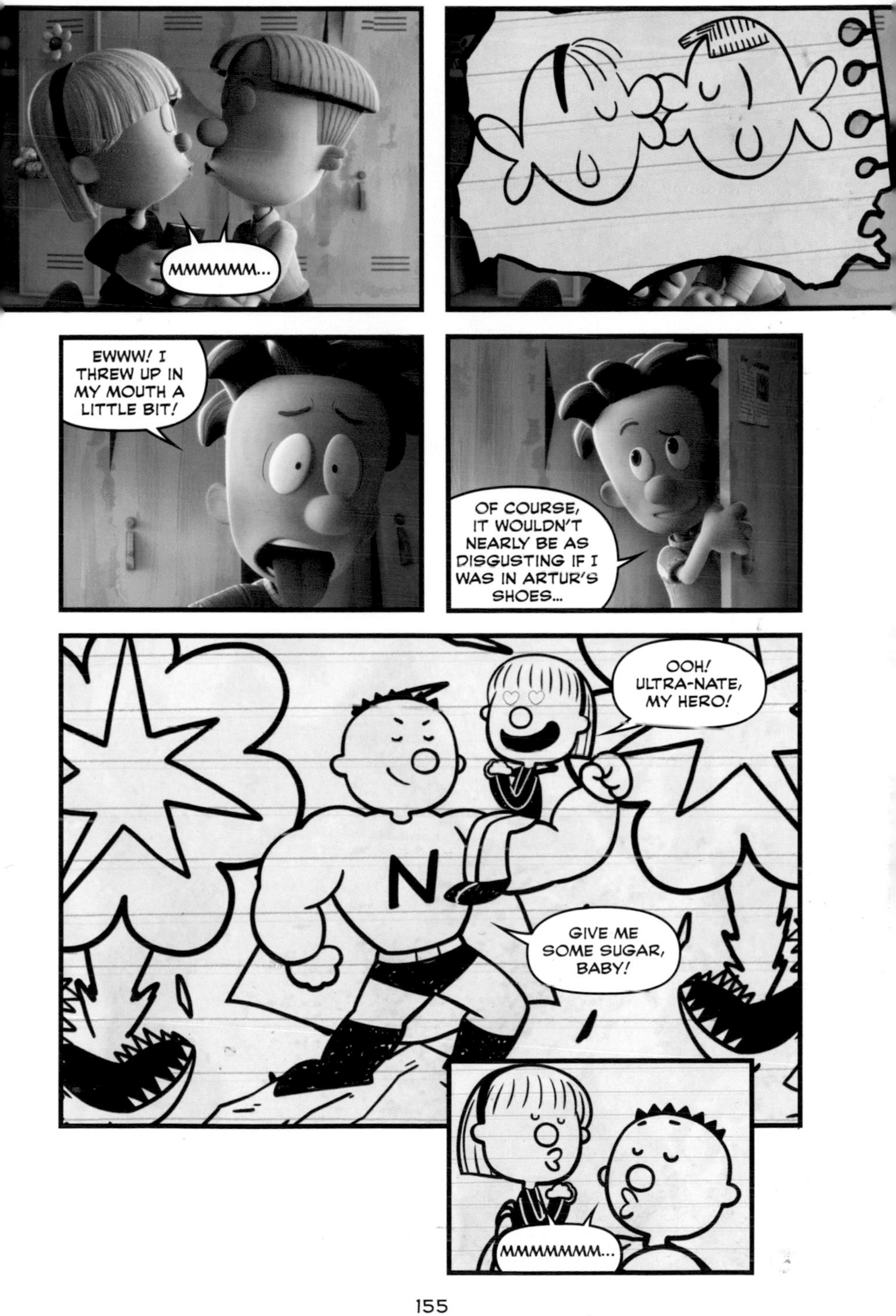

OOH! ULTRA-NATE, MY HERO!

GIVE ME SOME SUGAR, BABY!

MMMMMMM...

I LOVE YOU,
MY LITTLE MALL
FOOD COURT
CINNAMON BUN!

I LOVE YOU TOO, BRO. BUT NOT
IN A LIP LOCK SORT OF WAY.
AND ONLY MY ***MOM*** CALLS ME
"CINNAMON BUN."
HAHA!
WHAT IN THE
WORLD?

ALL RIGHT LAUGH IT
UP, KNUCKLEHEADS!
HAHA!

ALL I KNOW IS, JENNY'S GOING TO
GO TOTALLY NUTS FOR ME WHEN SHE
SEES ME SINGING IN THE BAND!

IF BY NUTS YOU MEAN
DRIVEN TO MADNESS BY
YOUR BOWEL-CLENCHING
SCREECHES...
WAIT,
WHAT?
NOTHING!

HEY, SPEAKING OF FEAR THE MOLLUSK, I THINK WE'RE READY TO RELEASE OUR ***AWESOMENESS*** ON THE WORLD!
WHAT DO YOU SAY, GUYS?

YOU MEAN, LIKE, PLAY IN FRONT OF ACTUAL PEOPLE, WITH OPINIONS AND EARS AND THE ABILITY TO THROW THINGS?

NO, IN FRONT OF SOCK PUPPETS. ***YES,*** ACTUAL PEOPLE! WHO ELSE?

I DON'T KNOW...

...IF THEY CAN HANDLE THE ***AWESOMENESS!*** GREAT IDEA, NATE!

THANKS, DEE DEE!
ALL RIGHT. NEXT STOP: ***SUPERSTARDOM!***
F

SEE YOU GUYS AT PRACTICE!

WE HAVE TO COME CLEAN WITH NATE. TELL HIM HIS SINGING SUCKS.
MMHMM!

LATER.

ARE YOU MARTIN?

...OF PETER, PAUL AND MARTIN, AMERICA'S **FAVORITE** ADULT CONTEMPORARY FOLK TRIO? I'M A **HUGE FAN!**
A MAN ISN'T A MAN UNTIL HE'S USED A PUBLIC BATHROOOOOM...

THAT GUITAR SOLO YOU DID AT THE FRIER-KATZ WEDDING WAS **OFF-THE-CHAIN MELLOW!**
THAT'S... WOW... I'M VERY TOUCHED!

WHAT BRINGS YOU TO P.S. 38?

I'M HERE TO PICK UP MY SON, NATE WRIGHT. DO YOU KNOW HIM?

KNOW HIM? HE'S ONLY MY MOST CREATIVE STUDENT! BUT I GUESS IT RUNS IN HIS BLOOD.

HOPEFULLY **UNEMPLOYMENT** DOESN'T RUN IN HIS BLOOD, TOO.

HEY NOW, NO FROWNY FACE. WE CREATIVE TYPES HAVE TO STICK TOGETHER.
I WORK FOR THIS **CATERING** COMPANY ON THE SIDE.

TEACHING FEEDS MY SOUL, BUT CATERING FEEDS MY FAMILY!
YOU SHOULD GIVE THEM A CALL!

THANKS!
DAD? DAD?

WHAT ARE YOU...? ≥SIGH.≤ YOU LOST YOUR JOB AGAIN.

ERR, YES...BUT I'VE GOT A NEW JOB! YOU'LL **NEVER** GUESS WHAT IT IS!

AW, C'MON, GIVE ME A HINT!

IT STARTS WITH A C...

C...C.E.O.?!

YOU'RE THE BIG BOSS?! DAD, THAT'S HUGE! I'M SO PROUD OF YOU!

I'M SO PROUD OF ME, TOO! FOR BEING A C.E.O.!

...WHICH IS WHAT I AM!

HEY, WHAT ARE YOU GUYS DOING HERE?

WE NEED TO TALK.
THREE GRUELING HOURS LATER...
YOU GUYS GOTTA BE *KIDDING* ME!

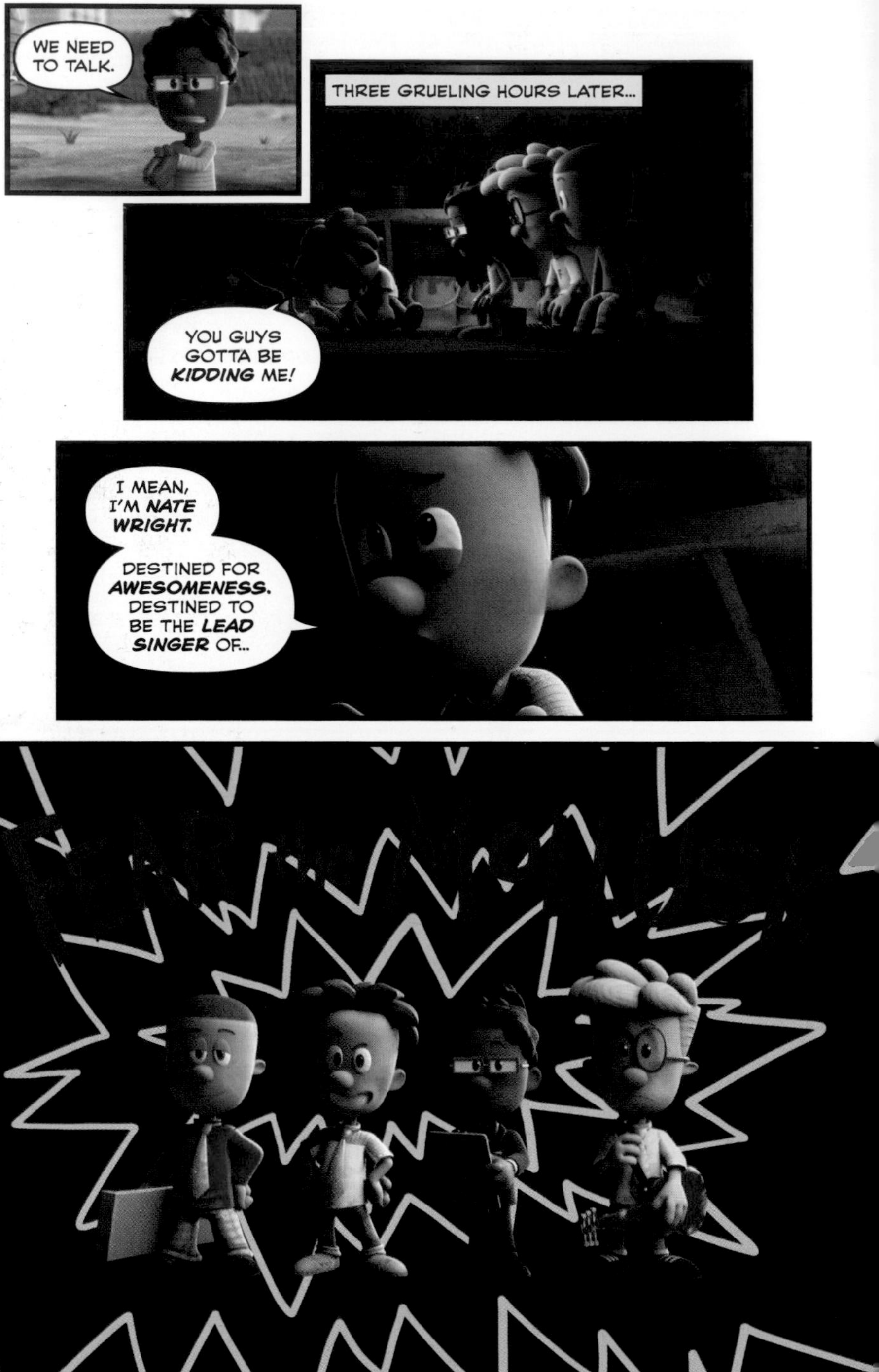

I MEAN, I'M *NATE WRIGHT.*
DESTINED FOR *AWESOMENESS.* DESTINED TO BE THE *LEAD SINGER* OF...

WE KNOW YOUR NAME! WE ALSO KNOW YOU'RE IN TOTAL DENIAL.

OBSERVE.
CLICK!

HEY, WOW! WE SOUND GREAT!

CAFETERIA MUSH, CAFETERIA MUSH, YOU'RE A STICKY MYSTERY TO ME THAT I LOVE TO EAT...

WHAT IS THAT SOUND?

AN OWL CHOKING ON A CHICKEN BONE? BAGPIPES IN A MICROWAVE?

YOU'RE GOOEY AND HARD, SPICY AND BLAND! WHY I'D WANT TO EAT YOU I JUST DON'T UNDERSTAND... OOOOOH, OOOOOOH!
A MANATEE GETTING HIT BY A BOAT PROPELLER?!

IT'S ***YOU,*** NATE! FOR THE LOVE OF ALL THINGS SACRED! IT'S ***YOU, SINGING!***

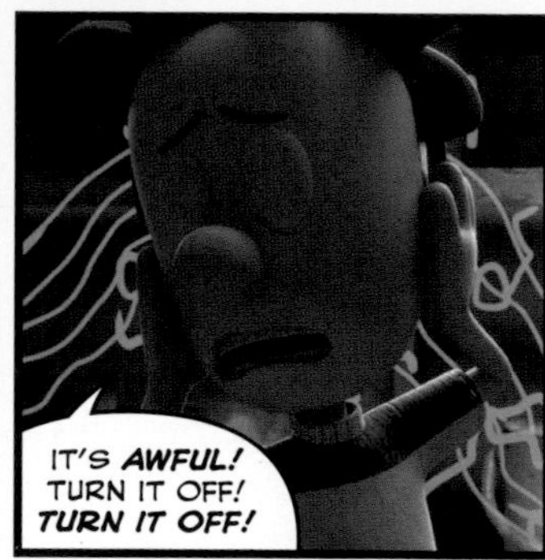
IT'S ***AWFUL!*** TURN IT OFF! ***TURN IT OFF!***

OKAY, FINE, YOU GUYS WIN! WE'LL HOLD LEAD SINGER AUDITIONS TOMORROW AFTER SCHOOL.

ALL RIGHT!
NOW YOU'RE TALKING SENSE!
GOOD MAN!

BUT WE'LL ONLY SETTLE FOR THE ***BEST!***

NOW THIS PERSON MUST HAVE ROCK STAR CHARISMA, KILLER DANCE MOVES, AND MOST IMPORTANTLY...

...***MIND-BOGGLING*** SINGING CHOPS.

OR JUST BE BETTER THAN YOU!

WE'LL SEE.

Chapter 2
EMERGENCY BAND HUDDLE

RESUME

HiRE ME!

Martin Wright
SKILLZ

• Pointing (Left AND right hande

C...E...O?

I'M THE C.E.O.

UNDERSTOOD! 10-4. NOT TRYING TO STEAL YOUR JOB. BUT...IS THERE *ANOTHER* C.E.O. SPOT? LIKE CUTLERY...EXPERT... OPERATOR?

WE'RE HIRING FOR A TEMPORARY CATERING POSITION.

I'LL TAKE IT!

I HAVEN'T OFFERED IT TO YOU YET.

YOU WON'T BE SORRY!
HONK!

I KIND OF ALREADY AM.

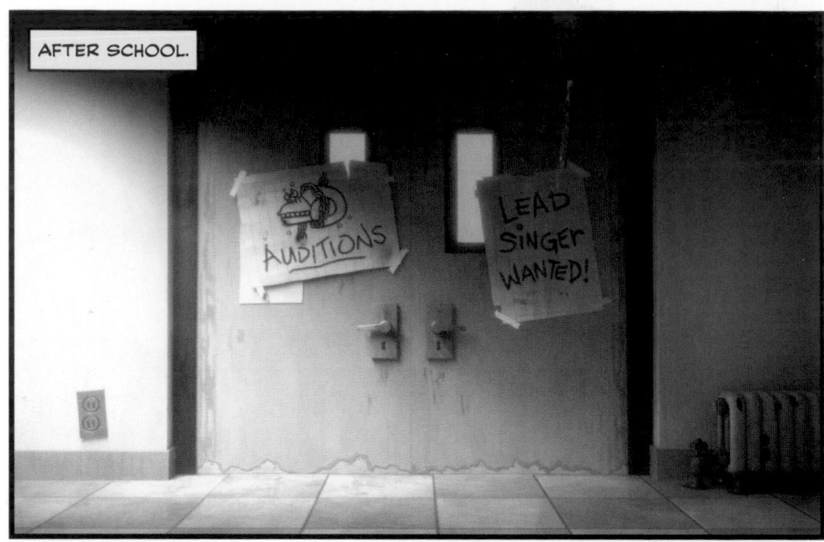
AFTER SCHOOL.
AUDITIONS
LEAD SINGER WANTED!

AS YOUR **MANAGER,** NATE, I'M REALLY PROUD OF YOU FOR PUTTING YOUR EGO ASIDE FOR THE SAKE OF THE BAND!
YEAH, YEAH, LET'S JUST GET THIS OVER WITH.

HOME, HOME ON THE RANGE...

NO.

RAH RAH
OOH RAH
RAH...

NO!

THE WHEELS ON
THE BUS GO
ROUND AND
ROUND...

NO!

NO!!

AWW.

THERE'S A
SQUIRREL
IN THE NUT
HOUSE...
NOOOO.

TASTY-
TASTE!
NO.

NO.

NO. NO.

NYET.

NEIN.

NO-NO-
NO-NO-

...MAYBE-
WAIT FOR
IT...

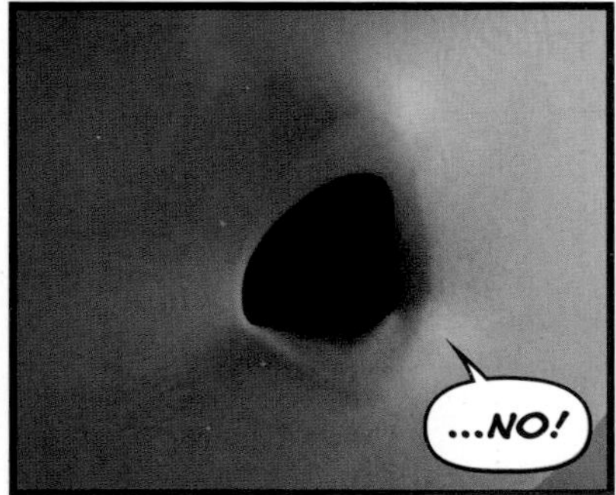
...NO!

ELSEWHERE...
ALL RIGHT, NEW GUY, LET'S START YOUR TRAINING.

I NEED YOU TO TAKE THAT TRAY AND SERVE EVERY DUMMY AT THAT TABLE THEIR BUBBLY. AND BY "BUBBLY," I MEAN GINGER-ALE.

NO PROBLEM!

GRUNT!

GRRR!

POP!

PFFFFFFT!

PLOP!

GLUG!
GLUG!

OH, SORRY SIR!
HERE, LET ME GIVE YOU MY SHIRT.

UM, HOLD ON! EASY... EEEAASY... *PHEW!*

WHAM!

GASP!
THUMP!

EASY...
EASY...
WOBBLE!
WOBBLE!

WHEW!

KRASH!

SCHLINK!

SCHLINK!

OH MY,
WHAT HAVE
I DONE?!
PFFFFT!

SOOOO, HOW'D I DO?

HOW WOULD YOU FEEL ABOUT WORKING IN THE BATHROOM?

I'LL DO IT!

MEANWHILE.
PS38

WELL, IT WAS WORTH A SHOT. GUESS I'M STILL OUR BEST OPTION, THOUGH.

HMM... OH! WHAT ABOUT DEE DEE?

OH, NO NO NO ***NO*** NO! MY VOICE IS AN ***INSTRUMENT*** TO BE USED ***STRICTLY*** FOR THE THEATER!

ALL RIGHT! WELL, THEN, IT'S SETTLED!
NOW IF YOU'LL EXCUSE ME, I HAVE SOME IMPORTANT BUSINESS TO TAKE CARE OF.

HA! MY CHARMINGLY STUBBORN PLAN TO STAY LEAD SINGER IS WORKING LIKE A–

WE STYLGRAVIANS ARE FEARFUL PEOPLE!
...HUH?!

UNQUESTIONABLY DEVOTED TO OUR MOTHERLAND...
UHH?

W-W-WAIT A MINUTE, I ONLY KNOW ONE STYLGRAVIAN.

OH **NO, NO, NO, N–**

IS THAT SOMEONE SINGING?
WHAT IS THAT SWEET SOUND?
OH, ES **PERFECTO.**

NO, NO,
NO, NO!

UH, HEY.

UH, WHOOPS!
ZIP!

WHAT'S UP,
GUYS?

NATE, WAS THAT
YOU SINGING?

OH, AH, YOU
COULD HEAR
THAT? UH, YEAH!
YEAH YEAH. UH-
HUH. THAT-THAT
WAS ME.

WE STYLGRAVIANS...

...ARE FEARFUL PEOPLE...
GROAN!

FRIEND NATE! YOU KNOW THE STYLGRAVIAN NATIONAL ANTHEM?!

ARTUR, I HAD TO CHECK MY PULSE TO MAKE SURE I DIDN'T DIE, BECAUSE YOU HAVE THE VOICE OF AN *ANGEL!*
WHERE'D YOU LEARN TO SING LIKE THAT?

S38
Public School of Extraordinary Excellence
HMPH.

ALWAYS I HAVE SING LIKE THAT!

IN MY VILLAGE IN STYLGRAVIA, WHENEVER THE GOATS WERE GETTING NERVOUS, MY SINGING WOULD SOOTHE THEM INTO PEACEFUL SLUMBER.

WHY WERE THE GOATS SO NERVOUS?

THEY WERE ABOUT TO BE SACRIFICED.
F

EMERGENCY BAND HUDDLE!

ARE YOU THINKING WHAT I'M THINKING?
THAT ARTUR SMELLS LIKE HAM?

NO! THAT WE SHOULD TOTALLY ASK ARTUR TO BE LEAD SINGER OF FEAR THE MOLLUSK!
TOTALLY!
100% WITH YOU!

WHOA, WHOA, WHOA. AREN'T YOU GUYS FORGETTING SOMETHING? ARTUR IS MY NEMESIS! HELLOOO?

HALLO, FRIEND NATE!

HE'S ALSO SUPER ANNOYING...
I DON'T THINK SO.
I LIKE ARTUR.
HE'S REALLY COOL.

ANNNND...HE'S WITH JENNY!

GASP!

SO?

SO?! I SHOULD BE WITH JENNY!

I THINK JENNY SHOULD BE WITH WHOEVER JENNY WANTS TO BE WITH!

ALL IN FAVOR OF ASKING ARTUR TO BE OUR LEAD SINGER, SAY AYE.

AYE!

ARRGH! *FINE.* I'LL DO WHAT THE BAND WANTS...EVEN THOUGH THE BAND IS MAKING A ***GINORMOUS*** MISTAKE!!

ARTUR, HOW WOULD YOU LIKE TO BE LEAD SINGER IN OUR BAND?

REALLY? YOU MEAN THIS?!

IN ARTUR COUNTRY, CRYING IS FORBIDDEN BECAUSE OTHERWISE WE WOULD NEVER STOP.
AWWWW...

HEY, ARTUR, BEING THE LEAD SINGER IN A BAND IS A ***BIG RESPONSIBILITY!*** SO, Y'KNOW, IF YOU WANT TO BACK OUT, NOW WOULD BE THE TIME...

I WILL NOT LET YOU DOWN, FRIEND NATE!

"AND IF I AM NOT DELIVER, I DEMAND TO RECEIVE TRADITIONAL STYLGRAVIAN PUNISHMENT FOR FAILURE: PUBLIC SHAVING FOLLOWED BY NO HUGS FOR A MONTH."

WELL, ***THAT*** WON'T BE NECESSARY. ALL YOU HAVE TO DO IS SHOW UP AT PRACTICE! WE'RE MEETING AT NATE'S HOUSE AT 5!
F

HOKAY! WILL BE THERE! SEEING YOU LATER, FRIENDS!

WOW! SMART, HANDSOME, AND A SINGER IN A BAND? NO **WONDER** JENNY'S MADLY IN LOVE WITH HIM!

BANG! BANG!
HE'LL BE ALL RIGHT...

Chapter 3
PROJECT ROCK GOD

MUNCH!
CRUNCH!

MARTY'S GOT HIMSELF A NEW JOB!

NEW JOB? I THOUGHT YOU JUST BECAME A C.E.O.!
OH, UH...

REMEMBER, MARTIN, YOU ALREADY TOLD HIM YOU WERE A C.E.O. KEEP UP WITH THE RUSE! GIVE HIM SOMETHING TO BELIEVE IN!

UH...WHY, ***YES!*** YOU ***ARE*** LOOKING AT A NEW C.E.O.!
THAT'S GREAT, DAD! WHEN DO YOU START?

RING! RING!
UH... HOLD THAT THOUGHT.

HELLO? OH, HI! TOMORROW? THE MAYER-SAFERSON WEDDING? SHOOT, MY BAND WAS SUPPOSED TO PLAY THAT WEDDING.
YOU DON'T CARE? YES, OF COURSE I UNDERSTAND.

C.E.O. BUSINESS?

SORRY, SON! I HAVE TO MAKE A FEW CALLS.

THIS IS MARTIN WRIGHT. I'M REALLY SORRY, BUT YOU'RE GOING TO HAVE TO FIND A NEW BAND FOR THE WEDDING. YES, I KNOW IT'S LAST MINUTE...

BUT NOT TOO LATE FOR ME TO BECOME AN INTERNATIONAL ROCK SENSATION!

HEY, PETER, I HATE TO BE THE BEARER OF BAD NEWS, BUT—

...I'M GOING TO DRAW A LUKEWARM BATH. PAPA NEEDS PAMPERING!

HEH HEH HEH!

* 0 #
FLASH
REDIAL

OKAY, NATE, DEEP VOICE...≥AHEM!≤
YES, I HEARD YOU'RE LOOKING FOR A BAND TO PLAY AT YOUR WEDDING TOMORROW?

ALL RIGHT, PROJECT **NATE WRIGHT IS A ROCK GOD** IS BACK ON!

KWANNG!

HALLO, FRIEND NATE!

JUST NEED TO TAKE CARE OF **MR. PERFECT** OVER THERE.

OH, HELLO, ARTUR! DID YOU FIND MY HOUSE OKAY?

WAS SUPER EASY. I JUST FOLLOW HOWLS OF DESPAIR FROM YOUR FAITHFUL HOUND!

AWOOOOO!

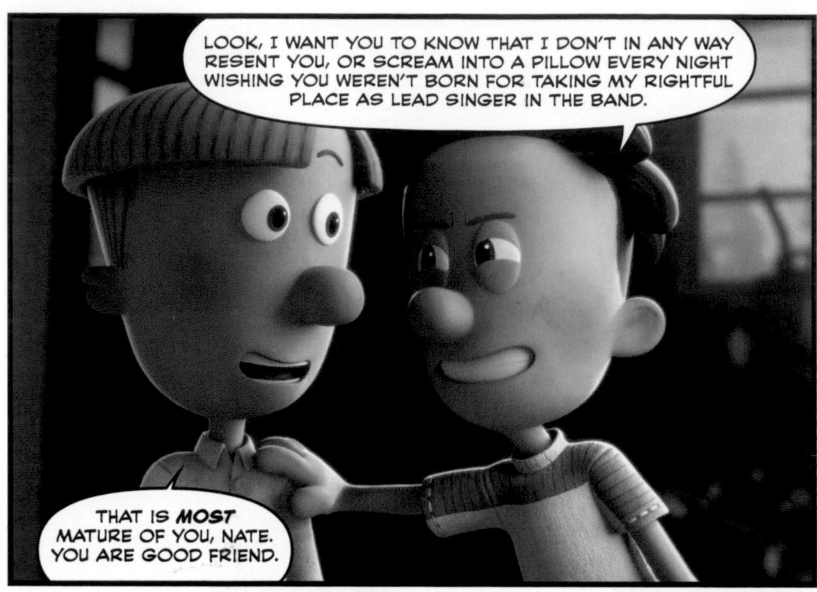
LOOK, I WANT YOU TO KNOW THAT I DON'T IN ANY WAY RESENT YOU, OR SCREAM INTO A PILLOW EVERY NIGHT WISHING YOU WEREN'T BORN FOR TAKING MY RIGHTFUL PLACE AS LEAD SINGER IN THE BAND.
THAT IS *MOST* MATURE OF YOU, NATE. YOU ARE GOOD FRIEND.

YEAH, YEAH, YEAH. AND GOOD FRIENDS, LIKE US, SHOULD REALLY KNOW EACH OTHER'S WEAKNESSES!
LIKE MY WEAKNESS IS... NOTHING!

DO *YOU* HAVE ANY WEAKNESSES I SHOULD KNOW ABOUT, FRIEND ARTUR?

WELL, TO TELL TRUTH, I ONLY SING IN PRIVATE BEFORE. OR TO GOATS!
IN MY VILLAGE IN STYLGRAVIA, IT IS BELIEVED THAT ANYTIME THERE IS IMMODEST SINGING...

STYLGRAVIA!
"...IT ATTRACTS A LEGENDARY TWO-HEADED BEAST CALLED THE AZDAYA WHO EATS OUR LOVED ONES!"
CHOMP!

ROAAAAAARRR!

OH, YEAH, I CAN ***DEFINITELY*** USE THIS!

OM NOM NOM!
WHATCHA DOIN', CHAD?

COLLECTING NUTS BEFORE THE SQUIRRELS GET THEM ALL!

YEAH, GOOD THINKING. SO, I NEED YOU TO DO ME A LITTLE FAVOR...

HEY, ARTUR, WHAT'S UP?!
OH, NOTHING, JUST WAITING. WE STYLGRAVIANS ARE KNOWN FOR OUR WAITING.

OKAY, EVERYONE, OKAY! THANK YOU FOR COMING.

I HAVE A VERY IMPORTANT ANNOUNCEMENT TO MAKE.
I GOT US A *GIG!*

WE'RE GOING TO BE PLAYING A VERY PUBLIC WEDDING...

GASP!

VERY PUBLIC...

WHIMPER!

...*TOMORROW!*

THIS COULDN'T BE BETTER TIMED. I JUST GOT YOU ALL NEW OUTFITS!
F

UM, DEE DEE, WHAT AM I TO SING?

OH, RIGHT! SORRY, ARTUR. HMM. HOW'S YOUR SIGHT READING?

EXCELLENT!

HMMPH!

PERFECT! HERE YOU GO.

ALL RIGHT THEN! EVERYONE! AH ONE, TWO, THREE!

CAFETERIA MUSH, CAFETERIA MUSH, YOU'RE A STICKY MYSTERY TO ME THAT I LOVE TO EAT.

GOOEY AND HARD. SPICY AND BLAND. WHY I'D WANT...

OH, NO! IT'S THE ***AZDAYA!*** ARTUR, ***RUN!***

GRRRRRRR!

EEEEK!

WELL, THAT WAS SURPRISINGLY EASY!

WHAT WAS THAT ALL ABOUT?
ARTUR PROBABLY JUST GOT STAGE FRIGHT!

YOU SEE, DEE DEE? BEING LEAD SINGER TAKES A CERTAIN KIND OF *JE NE SAIS QUAT*...

YOU KNOW WHAT, NATE? YOU'RE **RIGHT!**
WE'VE BEEN SO FOCUSED ON YOUR ***TOTALLY AWFUL*** SINGING, WE'VE OVERLOOKED YOUR ***LEADERSHIP...***
...AND ***TRUSTWORTHINESS.***

YEAH, AND THE WAY YOU'D NEVER, **EVER,** TRICK ANYONE INTO LEAVING THE BAND, **NATE!**

OKAY, THAT LAST ONE WAS ODDLY SPECIFIC.

WE'LL SUPPORT YOU, EVEN THOUGH YOUR SINGING SHOULD ONLY BE USED AS A DETERRENT DURING A NATIONAL EMERGENCY!

BECAUSE THAT'S WHAT BAND MEMBERS DO. THEY **SUPPORT** EACH OTHER!

FRANCIS MADE A GOOD POINT THERE, BRO. HOPE YOU WERE LISTENING!
W-W-W-WAIT, HEY! SHOULDN'T WE KEEP PRACTICING?

GRRRR!

WAS THE GROWLING TOO OVER THE TOP?

YOU DID GOOD, PAL.

FLICK!
MMM!

Chapter 4
SHOWTIME!

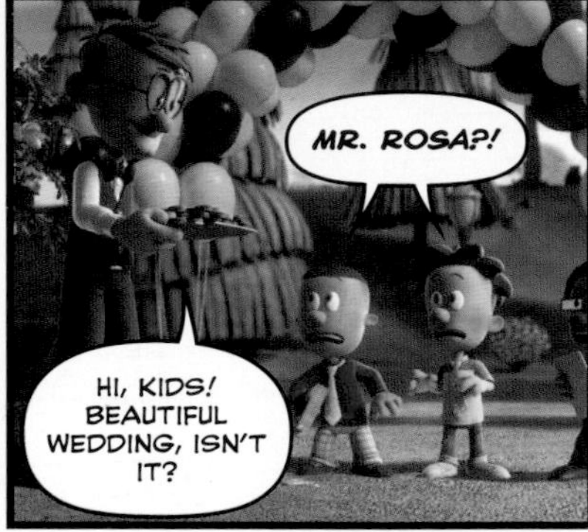

BUT YOU SAID YOU PLAYED THE GRAMMYS!

WELL, TECHNICALLY THAT'S TRUE! MY GRAMMY LOVES IT WHEN I PLAY THE DRUMS FOR HER!

SLAP!

I *KNEW* IT SOUNDED TOO GOOD TO BE TRUE! JUST DON'T EAT ANY OF THE FOOD, OKAY?

IF YOU SAY SO.
PTOO!

SPLUT!
MORE, PLEASE!

DAD?!

NATE?
NATE! WHAT ARE YOU GUYS DOING HERE?

OH, WELL... WE'RE THE NEW BAND!
WELL, THIS IS **GREAT!** I GET TO HEAR MY SON'S BAND PLAY THEIR FIRST GIG!
YEAH, AND I GET TO SEE MY DAD C.E.O.-ING. WAIT, THAT'S NOT REALLY A VERB, IS IT?

WHY DO YOU HAVE TO BE HERE, ANYWAY?
I THOUGHT YOU WERE THE **BOSS!**

I AM! YOU THERE! KEEP DOING WHAT YOU'RE DOING!

CRASH!

AND... CLEAN UP THAT MESS!

WELL, I BETTER GO BOSS SOME MORE PEOPLE AROUND. KNOCK 'EM DEAD, SON!

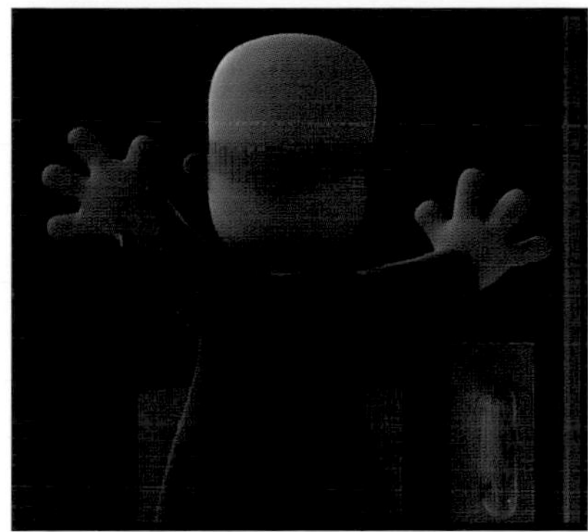

PHEW!
THAT WAS CLOSE!

CAFETERIA MUSH ON THREE! AH ONE, TWO, THREE!

YOU LOOK SO BEAUTIFUL RIGHT NOW.

CAFETERIA MUSH, CAFETERIA MUSH, YOU'RE A STICKY MYSTERY TO ME...

AHHHHH!

...THAT I LOVE TO EAT, YOU'RE GOOEY AND HARD. SPICY AND BLAND, WHY I'D WANT TO EAT YOU I DON'T UNDERSTAND...
KSSSCCHH!

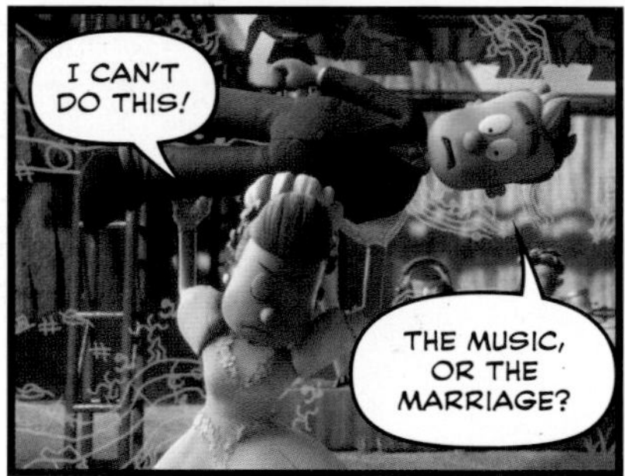
I CAN'T DO THIS!
THE MUSIC, OR THE MARRIAGE?

BOTH!

OOOOOH OOOOOH!

BOOM!
AHHHHH!
CRASH!

OH, MY GOSH, GUYS, WHAT DO WE DO?!

GUYS?

GUYS?!

OH, GEEZ, OH, N-NO, OH, GEEZ...

...WHAT HAVE I DONE?!

MEANWHILE.
TRUST ME, A SUCCESSFUL RELATIONSHIP HAS ***NOTHING*** TO DO WITH LOVE.

AHHH! DAD? WHAT ARE YOU ***DOING*** IN HERE?

ME? OH, JUST WASHING MY HANDS! AS ONE DOES IN A BATHROOM!

THANKS FOR THE BRO TALK, DUDE. YOU'RE REALLY GOOD AT YOUR JOB!

DAD, WHY DID THAT STRANGE MAN JUST PAY YOU FOR A MOIST TOWELETTE AND A PEPPERMINT?

WELL..UM... BECAUSE...I...UH...I'M NOT A C.E.O! I COULDN'T EVEN HACK IT AS AN APPRENTICE CATERER. I'M A–

TOWEL BOY.

ACTUALLY MY TITLE IS **BATHROOM ATTENDANT!** ANYWAY, I JUST WANTED YOU TO BE PROUD OF YOUR OLD MAN! I'M SORRY I LIED TO YOU, NATE.

NO, NO, IT'S OKAY! LOOK, IF WE'RE BEING HONEST, I'M NOT A PERFECT SINGER—I MEAN I'M **GOOD,** DUH, BUT MORE OF AN **ACQUIRED TASTE!** AHEAD OF MY TIME!
BUT YOU'RE A GREAT DRUMMER! SOMETIMES WE HAVE TO ACCEPT THE THINGS WE'RE BAD AT...
NEVER SAID I WAS BAD!

...TO SEE WHAT WE'RE REALLY **GOOD** AT! FOR ME, THAT'S HANDING PEOPLE TOWELS AND PLAYING THERAPIST TO MEN IN NICE SUITS!

DAD, THERE'S SOMETHING I GOTTA DO.

GO GET 'EM, TIGER!

MARTY, WE UH...
NEED YOU IN
THE WOMEN'S
RESTROOM. IT'S
THE BRIDE...

SAY NO
MORE! I'M
ON IT.

TOWEL
BOY

AHHHH!

WHAM!
CRUNCH!

OH, FRIEND NATE! IT IS JUST YOU!

I THOUGHT IT WAS THE AZDAYA AGAIN! FACE ME, CREATURE BORN OF MUD AND SULLIED VEGETATION! I RIGHT HERE!

ARTUR, LOOK, THAT WASN'T THE AZDAYA. IT WAS JUST CHAD!

WHAT?

I WAS JEALOUS OF YOU AND YOUR BONKERS-AMAZING SINGING VOICE, AND FOR DATING JENNY—STILL NOT GONNA LET THAT LAST ONE GO—BUT FOR NOW, WE NEED YOU, ARTUR. WE NEED YOU TO SING.

HOKAY, WELL, I THINK ABOUT IT.

NO, ARTUR, YOU'RE NOT GETTING IT! WE LITERALLY NEED YOU TO SING RIGHT NOW!

SOB!
I CAN'T TELL YOU WHAT TO DO. I CAN ONLY TELL YOU THAT THE MAN OUT THERE LOVES YOU!

NOT JUST THE WOMAN HE MET AT BOBBY WESTON'S 26TH BIRTHDAY PARTY, BUT THE WOMAN YOU ARE *TODAY.*
THE WOMAN YOU'LL BE IN 10 YEARS. 30 YEARS. HECK, 50 YEARS!

YOU REALLY THINK SO?
I KNOW I *THINK* I THINK I *KNOW* SO.

THANK YOU.
I'M JUST DOIN' MY JOB.

RATTLE!
TIPS

OOH!
TIPS

ALWAYS THE BRIDESMAID, NEVER THE BRIDE! YEEEOOOH!

FOOOMM!

WOOSH!

FWIP!

THANK GOODNESS YOU'RE HERE! FRANCIS AND TEDDY HAVE BEEN CYCLING THROUGH THE SAME THREE SONGS AND THE GUESTS ARE GOING CRAZY!

THEN WE CAN'T DO ANY OF OUR REGULAR SONGS...

MAY I TAKE LIBERTY TO SING PRIVATE LOVE SONG I WROTE FOR JENNY?

NO! BARF.
NATE?!
FIIIINE.

HOKAY THEN...

IN THE KEY OF SHEEP!

IN MY TINY VILLAGE IN STYLGRAVIA...

I DREAM ABOUT A GIRL LIKE YOU...

EYES BRIGHT LIKE FLAMING GOATS, WE SACRIFICED FOR GOOD HARVEST OF OATS...LIPS SO SOFT, THEY CALL TO ME...

SNIFF!

...LIKE FRIENDLY SHEEP DOG... DEVOID OF FLEAS... OH, AMERICAN DREAM GIRL...

YOU ARE TO ME THE WHOLE WORLD, NO, NOT JUST A NEW START, YOU ARE MY PETTY CAPITALIST SWEETHEART...
I CAN'T CONTAIN MYSELF MUCH LONGER. CAN'T YOU HEAR MY HEART? GIRL, IT BEATS SO BRAZENLY...

...'CAUSE I LOVE YOU, IMMODESTLY. OHHH...

'CAUSE I LOVE YOU IMMODESTLY.

THE BRIDE IS MY COUSIN'S COUSIN, THRICE REMOVED. WE'RE A TIGHT-KNIT FAMILY. ARTUR, THAT WAS ***AMAZING!*** WHY DIDN'T YOU TELL ME YOU WERE IN A BAND?

I WAS ASHAMED OF MY SINGING...BUT MY FELLOW BANDMATES SHOW ME I HAVE NO REASON TO BE AFRAID.

ERR...HEH HEH...

UGH. OKAY, OKAY. MAYBE I DESERVE THIS.

OR MAYYYYBEEE...
ROOOOAR!

AHHHH!

MARRY ME
♡NATE♡

...I CAN WRITE MY OWN ENDING!

DEE DEE, I'M GOING TO ASK YOU A QUESTION, AND I WANT YOU TO BE COMPLETELY HONEST WITH ME.
WHO'S A BETTER SINGER: ME OR AR—
ARTUR.
ARTUR BY A MILE! ARTUR ALL DAY, EVERY DAY! IT'S NOT EVEN CLOSE!
I SAID TO BE HONEST, NOT VICIOUS.
I'M A RANDOM PASSERBY, AND I **ALSO** THINK ARTUR'S BETTER!
PEIRCE

F

SHOW CREDITS

WRITTEN BY
MITCH WATSON
ELLIOTT OWEN
SARAH ALLAN
ERIC SHAW

STORYBOARD ARTISTS
KAT CHAN
LAKE FAMA
HEATHER GREGERSEN
KIMBERLY JO MILLS
JIM MORTENSEN
JEFF DEGRANDIS
BRADLEY GOODCHILD
ZOË MOSS
KYLE NESWALD
KEVIN SINGLETON
GREY WHITE
SEBASTIAN DUCLOS
RAY GEIGER
BRANDON WARREN
MARIANA YOVANOVICH
MARIA NGUYEN
MEG SYVERUD
COLIN HECK
MIKE DOUGHERTY
VICTORIA HARRIS
BENJAMIN HOLM
TANNER JOHNSON

CONSULTING PRODUCER
LINCOLN PEIRCE

CO-PRODUCER
BRIDGET MCMEEL

ART DIRECTOR
DAVID SKELLY

CG SUPERVISOR
CHRISTINA LAFERLA

SUPERVISING PRODUCER
JIM MORTENSEN

PRODUCER
AMY MCKENNA

EXECUTIVE PRODUCER
JOHN COHEN

EXECUTIVE PRODUCER
MITCH WATSON
HEAD WRITER
EMILY BRUNDIGE
STAFF WRITERS
SARAH ALLAN
BEN LAPIDES

ASSOCIATE PRODUCER
TAYLOR BRADBURY
STORYBOARD REVISIONISTS
ANDREW CAPUANO
MISTY MARSDEN
JAZZLYN WEAVER

SCRIPT COORDINATOR
LISSY KLATCHKO
PRODUCTION COORDINATORS
BRANDON CHAU
CLAIRE NORRIS
CARLINA WILLIAMS
LOGAN YUZNA
SIENNA SERTL
ASSET PRODUCTION COORDINATORS
DIANA GRIGORIAN
SEAN MCPARTLAND

PRODUCTION ASSISTANTS
CYNTHIA CORTEZ
SARA FISHER
DARREN OJEDA
NATASHA SHIELDS
HANNAH JANE GOULDEN
CAITLYN KURILICH
AJ SHENEFELT
EXECUTIVE ASSISTANT
ALEX VAN DER HOEK

CHARACTER DESIGNERS
ROBERT BROWN
JUN LEE
JOCELYN SEPULVEDA
BACKGROUND DESIGNERS
PETER J. DELUCA
GRACE KUM
BECCA RAMOS
JOSH WESSLING
PROP DESIGNERS
ZACHARY CLARKSON
TYLER WILLIAM GENTRY
RC MONTESQUIEU
SHANNON PRESTON
2D DESIGNER
VICKI SCOTT
BACKGROUND PAINTERS
NATALIE FRANSCIONI-KARP
JONATHAN HOEKSTRA
QUINTIN PUEBLA
PATRICK MORGAN

LEAD CG GENERALIST
VYPAC VOUER
LEAD CHARACTER TECHNICAL DIRECTOR
AREEBA RAZA KHAN
LEAD LOOK DEVELOPMENT ARTIST
CANDICE STEPHENSON
LOOK DEVELOPMENT ARTIST
JUAN GIL

COLOR CORRECTION SERVICES
ROUNDABOUT ENTERTAINMENT
COLORIST
BRYAN MCMAHAN

CG GENERALIST
THOMAS THOMAS III

ANIMATION DIRECTOR
DENNIS SHELBY
MARK LEE
LIGHTING & COMPOSITING DIRECTOR
DARREN D. KINER
CODY BURKE
ASSOCIATE ART DIRECTOR
SAM KOJI HALE

2D ANIMATION SERVICES
XENTRIX TOONS
FOR XENTRIX TOONS
CREATIVE DIRECTOR
HARRIS CABEROY
PRODUCTION MANAGER
SHERYLEN CAOILI
FX SUPERVISOR
KERWIN OJO
PRODUCTION TEAM
ARA KATRIN LUDOVICO
JANILLE BIANCA TUDELA

SPECIAL THANKS
BRIAN ROBBINS
RAMSEY NAITO
BRIAN KEANE
ANGELIQUE YEN
DANA CLUVERIUS
CLAUDIA SPINELLI

ANIMATION DEVELOPMENT
NATHAN SCHRAM
LESLIE WISHNEVSKI

CURRENT SERIES MANAGEMENT
NEIL WADE

VICE PRESIDENT OF ANIMATION PRODUCTION
DEAN HOFF

EXECUTIVE IN CHARGE FOR NICKELODEON
NATHAN SCHRAM

Joi
MATH
IT "ADD
TO F

Complete Your *Big Nate* Collection